NIGHT TRAIN

Donald O'Donovan

Published by Open Books 2013

Cover art by Aaron Quinn

ISBN: 0615722830
ISBN-13: 978-0615722832

1

I WAS DOING MY LAUNDRY in the men's room of the all-night movie theater on South Broadway, and who walks in but Jack? Little Jack with the red hat... Tony's Jack! It was Friday, last week, or was it Saturday? I'm wringing out my socks in the sink, and he's tapping me on the shoulder. Jack was a mess. His clothes were ragged and dirty, and his red hat was full of stickers. He'd been sleeping out with the coyotes. And no Tony.

I put my things in a plastic garbage bag and we went back out, sat down and shared a bag of stale popcorn. We managed to catch a few winks, and in the morning, over coffee at Grand Central Market, he told me the story. Or he tried to tell it. The quality woman...the mansion in Brentwood. The words came out of him helter-skelter, like the song of a bird, a bird beaten down by a storm, a bird that had swallowed a poisoned worm. They were working the crowd in front of Bullocks Wilshire. Tony was sitting on his regular bus bench. Then the quality woman from Brentwood got her hooks into the big handsome guy. She kidnapped him. She adopted him.

I first met Jack and Tony several months before on Fifth Street. It was raining. Jack was a pipsqueak with a sinister black widow's peak, conning black eyes and a

1

pirate's toothy grin. Tony was six feet tall, well built, and graceful on his feet, with huge hands. He was strangely silent.

"Tony, this is—what's your name?"

"Jerzy. Jerzy Mulvaney."

"Jerzy, this is Tony. Tony, this is Jerzy."

We stood under a liquor store awning to get out of the drizzle. The owner came out and told us to move on. We ended up at Clifton's. We had enough for coffee. It was Jack who did all the talking.

"Do you know who this is?" Jack asked me. He kept plucking at my sleeve.

"Yeah, sure, he's Tony."

"He's Tony, yeah, but Tony who? Do you know who this is? This is Tony Canzoneri. He fought Jake LaMotta in the Garden."

"Tony Canzoneri?"

"Yeah, Tony Canzoneri. This is Tony Canzoneri."

I shook hands again with Tony—my hand disappeared in his—then he sank back in his chair, as if the effort of meeting me had exhausted him. They were a great combination, the famous fighter on the skids and his peppery little promotion man. It was a good story. But there were holes in it. This Tony guy was obviously an athlete but he must have fought LaMotta when he was a baby because Jake LaMotta is eighty-something now and this Tony looked to be only about forty-five or fifty tops.

When Tony got up to go to the toilet I plied Jack with questions.

"What's the matter with him? Why doesn't he talk?"

"Punchy." Jack tapped his forehead. "He's punchy. Say, you wanna get on a wine? I've got seventy-six cents."

Later I looked up Tony Canzoneri at a wifi on Fairfax. Tony Canzoneri was a lightweight and LaMotta was a middleweight. They never fought. Besides, Tony Canzoneri passed away in 1959.

Weeks or months went by and I ran into Tony and Jack

again, this time by Bullocks Wilshire. They were coming on to the tourists. Jack, wearing a little red mountaineer's hat, was expertly working the crowd while Tony lounged seductively on a bus bench like a big tawny tiger. Jack and Tony. They were raking it in. There's no getting around it, I thought, this Tony's got charisma up the ass. The tourists couldn't take their eyes off him. They clustered around his bus bench, snapping photos and begging for autographs. I kept out of the way. I didn't want to queer their deal. After things died down I went up to Jack. I wanted to see if he remembered me. He did, and so did Tony. Jack handed me a five spot right away—"for eats"—and then I grasped Tony's paw, that enormous strangely soft hand of his, like a padded tiger paw. Tony smiled faintly and murmured something like "*Buon Giorno.*" He kept pulling on a bottle, grimly, as if he had a horror of being sober. It was the hard stuff, a flat pint tightly wrapped in brown bag paper.

"Come on over to the park after a few," Jack said. "We're gonna score a jug."

I went to the Alexandria Jack in the Box for a Jumbo Jack and fries, but when I got back to Lafayette Park Jack and Tony had moved on.

AND NOW HERE WE WERE at Grand Central Market, Jack and I. We were hungry and we were dead broke, but the coffee was good, the waitress was pretty, and it was a brand new day.

"I didn't care much for the movie," Jack said.

"*Night of the Living Dead?* Naw, it was pretty cheesy."

Grand Central Market. What a place. Nothing like it anywhere in the world. Strangled sea creatures lolling on beds of crushed ice, goggling like embryos torn from the womb. Glistening loaves of bread, steaming kettles of menudo, yellow wheels of cheese. The food! The smells! My God, it'll drive you crazy. And everywhere a buzzing of dialects, a babble of tongues. The dirty coins change hands, the mouths open and snap shut, the food goes down the gullet, the shopping bags are stuffed and the buyers totter off, conversing in their own special lingo.

I tried to get Jack to come clean about Tony. I didn't want to tell him straight out that I never bought his story about Tony fighting Jake LaMotta in the Garden, so I just dropped a couple of hints. But Jack came up with another story. How much of it is true I can't say. Jack is almost certainly a pathological liar. It turns out that Tony had been a concert pianist in Italy. He played a gig in New York, but got drunk and wound up on the skids with Jack in LA. It was more complicated than that, but that was the broad outline of it.

"So he went to live in Brentwood with this, this..."

"This cunt? Yeah, she was older, you know, but pretty easy on the eyes. I went to see him but she didn't like me hanging around. Tony said he missed me but he had to look out for number one, you know? I mean, she was even talking about taking him to Paris with her."

"Sure. But there's something I've been wondering about."

"Yeah, what's that?"

"How come Tony never talks?"

"Well, he's Italian, for one thing. He's only got a few words of English. But the other thing is, well, he's deaf."

"Deaf? I thought you said he was a concert pianist."

"He is. He was, I mean. He reads the notes; you know what I'm saying? I don't know how he does it, but he does it. You should hear him play, man. He's a fucking virtuoso. If you got it you got it. I mean, Beethoven was deaf, wasn't he?"

Jack is a real survivor and plenty streetwise, but without Tony he was going nowhere fast. And he wasn't going to have any luck pimping me to the crowd. We both knew that well enough.

I told Jack that the best idea was to catch a bus up to Brentwood and get Tony away from the quality woman.

"Yeah, but that's the problem, you see. He ain't there

no more."

"What do you mean?"

"She dumped him. He's gone, man."

"How do you know?"

"The gardener. I was camping out for two weeks in these big old hydrangea bushes outside the gate. He'd come and hand me some grub through the bars, the gardener. Pretty decent guy, Japanese guy. Then yesterday he told me."

"She dumped him?"

"Yeah. It was the drinking. She couldn't handle it. Tony's a suicidal drinker, you know."

"I know."

"I figure he's playing piano in a bar somewhere now. That's what he was doing when I met him in New York. Jesus, that guy had a villa in Tuscany and shit. He was somebody. I mean he used to go foxhunting with the Prince of Wales. He was a racecar driver, too. I'm not shitting you. He went the distance with Mario Andretti at Le Mans. Then his daughter drowned in the pool and he started on the sauce. He got drunk before a concert and fucked up by the numbers on stage. We came out here on a freight."

"So what are you gonna do, Jack?"

"Find him! We gotta find him. We gotta find Tony, man."

"We? What do you mean, we?"

"Yeah, well, I was hoping you'd help me look for him…"

Jack, when you got to know him, was something of a bore. There'd been a woman back in New York, a dime-a-dance girl named Francine, and he couldn't stop talking about her. Francine broke his heart, and Francine this and Francine that, and it was Francine who drove him to drink, and all the rest of it. Their stories are all the same, these heartbroken guys, these side-of-the-road lonely boys, lonely and lost and stumbling drunk, and they go on and on until you want to put them out of their misery just like you'd do with a horse.

Jack's other subject, besides Francine, is the revolution. Jack believes in the revolution. And he thinks it's right around the corner.

"The poor will rise up like a river," he told me. "We'll yank the rich off their thrones and throw them to the dogs in the street. We'll empty their pockets, take their rings and watches and knock the gold out of their teeth with a baseball bat. *We have smitten the Philistines hip and thigh, baby!* They're goin' down! They're goin' down to Chinatown."

Chinatown… Chinatown reminds me of Ashlee because Phillipe's, on the edge of Chinatown, was our favorite restaurant, Ashlee's and mine. I've been thinking about Ashlee all day, so maybe I spoke too soon; I mean the things I just said about Jack. But it's a different scenario with me. I don't go around mooning over Ashlee the way Jack does with Francine. No way! I met Ashlee at the Dreamland Dance Club, Eighth and Spring, fourth floor. It's one of those places where you pay by the minute. This was back in the days when I had a credit card.

I remember the night I met her. I was feeling more than a little nervous as I ducked inside the place and blinked my eyes to get them used to the darkness. I needed a drink badly, but there was a sign that read, "No liquor allowed." Fortunately I had a half pint of Old Crow stashed in my coat pocket.

Standing in the foyer, I surveyed the lineup of bored butterflies sprawled insolently in chairs with their backs to the wall. *Scrumptious!* A few of the love-dolls were whirling around the floor with their victims. I wasn't at all sure how things worked at the Dreamland Dance Club. Should I buy a ticket at the desk or do I ask a girl to dance? *Nervous, nervous.* I ducked into the toilet and quickly chugged my half-pint of Old Crow. Nothing like a few belts of cheap strong hooch to grease the trolley.

It was Ashlee who came to my rescue. She took me by

the hand and led me to the dance floor. A moment later we were locked in a close embrace, swaying clumsily to the strains of "Only You".

They say the sun even shines on a dog's ass once in a while.

Ashlee said she was from Weehawken. Her accent was genuine, so I believed her. She'd come to California to make movies. But who didn't? She was pretty enough to make movies, I thought. Long blonde hair, bangs, blue eyes, great tits. She was wearing a purple mohair turtleneck. I was crazed, but I wanted to make a good impression so I tried to remember the Arthur Murray lessons I took back when I was a private in the Army. *How the hell do you do the foxtrot?*

Pretty soon Ashlee suggested that we sit one out and talk things over. We waltzed our way into a dark little alcove where there were couches and easy chairs. You sensed that there were other couples present but you couldn't see them. You could hear them breathing, but it was so god awful dark you couldn't tell what was going on. Which was probably just as well.

We sat on a couch, close together. Ashlee stuck her tongue in my mouth and we began to paw each other frantically. I reached up under her sweater and unhooked her bra. I felt her fumbling with the tab of my zipper.

For a small extra charge, she explained, she would "make me happy."

"How much?"

"Fifty bucks." But it had to be cash. You couldn't put it on the card.

"Fifty bucks?" I didn't have that much on me. Not even close.

"Twenty-five," she whispered. She already had her hand in my fly.

Fortunately I had twenty-seven dollars in my pocket. I gave her a twenty and a five, and she brought me to orgasm skillfully with her hand. It was over in seconds. I spritzed all over the front of her sweater.

I was happy all right. But she wasn't. She was pissed off because she couldn't work anymore that night. Not with that goo on her sweater. So I asked if I could take her home.

"Okay, yeah, yeah. I mean that's the fucking least you can do. *Jesus!*"

We went up to the desk and cashed out. It came to sixty bucks on the card, and I wrote in a nice tip for her. I was feeling pretty good. It had been a banner night for a guy who couldn't even do the foxtrot.

But things went off on a bum tangent when we got outside and she learned that I didn't have a car. But I had an answer for that. A taxi, of course. We got in the back and mushed it up, and she took a pint of sloe gin out of her purse, and then another one. We were both looped now, laughing and kissing and feeling each other up.

It turns out that your taxis from downtown LA to Venice Beach are goddamn pricey. I put it on the credit card, which pretty well maxed it out. I never had any intention of paying it, of course. Chase Manhattan, I think, was the name of the bank that had been foolish enough to send me a credit card in the mail. I guess they thought I was a responsible person.

Eventually Ashlee landed a dog food commercial. She deserved it, poor kid. It's not much fun being pawed by lonely desperate men five nights a week at the Dreamland Dance Club. She got her own place, on Alexandria, behind Chapman Market. From her upstairs window you could see the site of the old Ambassador Hotel.

Then she picked up some work making karaokes. The studio was in Burbank. They wanted American-looking girls with blonde hair and big tits. You worked from a very short script, a treatment, actually. They shot at the Santa Monica Pier, then at Malibu, then at the Bronson Caves, a medieval scenario with handsome knights on horseback and Ashlee as a mysterious damozel. She made good money while the gig lasted, but she had to do the director a sexual favor, and finally the director dumped her and she went back to Weehawken.

It strikes me that I should have gone back to Weehawken. I should have gone back to Weehawken years ago.

THIS MORNING Big Bluto announced that we have to recall four thousand bottles of Clove Capsules. E. coli. Or maybe he said salmonella. As if we gave a rat's ass. But I had to laugh. Big Bluto was squirming. He'll push us harder now, pay us less.

The dish soap in the lunchroom is half water. I noticed that today when I went to wash my hands. That's how cheap he is, Big Bluto. He fills the dish soap bottle with water when it gets half empty.

We get fifteen minutes for lunch. When the buzzer sounds—*bzzzt*—it's back to work.

This afternoon I figured out how to jam the labeling machine. You feed them in a little bit crooked; it chews them up. This gambit paid off in a five-minute break for me. I pretended I didn't know how to fix the machine so Ponlok helped me out. Ponlok worked in a sweatshop in Cambodia that was a hundred times worse than this one. He's chopping in tall cotton now. Always cheerful, Ponlok. No English. The Cambodians stick together, Ponlok, Samay, Chaya, Chan and Kiri, but they're friendly. There are about twenty-five of us here, the Cambodians, the Mexicans, Khamtai from Laos and Ana from Guatemala. I'm the only native English speaker—except Big Bluto, of course.

Ana from Guatemala is a perfect little angel. Always saying her beads. She prays to Maria del Rosario. Maria del Rosario is very big in Guatemala. Ana has taken religion as a shield and a comforter. Her prayers are protection from the ugliness of the world. She lives in a sort of chrysalis, a haven, a sanctuary manufactured from her dreams, where nothing can touch her. She probably learned that at the Starbuck's plantation in Guatemala where her wages were $1.25 a day.

Monday. Big Bluto is launching a big promotional campaign for Dr. Sharpe's New Improved Parasite Cleanse. He called us together in the lunchroom, waving Dr. Sharpe's book, *Human Parasites*. That's Bluto's Bible, his *Mein Kamph*. Roundworms, pinworms, *Demodex Folliculorum*. He's got their photos up on the wall in the lunchroom, much enlarged, mug shots of the culprits, mailed in by satisfied customers who dredged the creatures up from their intestines. A tapeworm thirty-four feet long, a hookworm with savage Dracula teeth, a giant liver fluke, a canine heartworm—easily as menacing, these public enemies, as John Dillinger or Pretty Boy Floyd. They sift their stools through a strainer, the customers. I'm not exaggerating. It's all outlined in Dr. Sharpe's book, how to go about it, with the strainer and all. These people are Dr. Sharpe's protégés. He encourages them to play in their shit.

2

IT'S A FUNNY WORLD. Last week I was sleeping under a bridge, and here I am today with a job and a paycheck. I'm not the biggest rat in the shithouse, but I'm one of them now. I'm a real person, putting in my hours, scratching for a living, just like every other motherfucker in Christendom.

It's funny too about the nostalgia. Already it's hitting me. The bridge, I mean. I'd spend the day sitting on the cool pickle weed under the bridge reading Krishnamurti and getting jacked up on Night Train or Wild Irish Rose. It was a peaceful place. There were coyotes in the stubble fields and junkyards on the other side of the chain link fence but they kept their distance. Just the same, you could hear them howling at night and you knew they were out there, camped on the edge of civilization, ready to sink their teeth into an unwary Siamese cat, a freshly bathed poodle or a plump white child.

Then Mungy Nuncie showed up. She looked like a big lumpy beach ball with legs. No arms, just little seal flippers. Little sea turtle fins. She looked like a sea turtle, in fact. She smelled like one too. We'd have birria tacos for breakfast, and off she'd go, turning tricks. There were some illegals working in a bean field on the other side of the freeway. I don't know how much they were able to cough up. It couldn't have been much but at least there were a lot of them. She had some white johns too, rich guys. They'd pick her up in their Lincolns and Cadillacs. It turns out that there are a lot of men in the world who are just dying to get it on with a deformed woman. "They love my little flippers," she told me. There was something wrong with her tits, too. They were flat as pancakes. But I guess everything worked fine down below because she usually came back with a bundle.

Before long she got hooked up with a doctor, a neurosurgeon. He'd pick her up in his BMW. He'd take her back to his crib and let her take a bath. I was glad of that because that girl had a wicked stink to her. This doctor was a flipper fetishist. He'd get naked, she told me, and she had to caress him all over with her little flippers. He'd usually squirt in a matter of minutes and then they'd go out to Baskin Robbins for banana splits. He was a decent guy, the doctor. The gig paid a hundred bucks plus eats.

Nostalgia! It'll eat you alive. Nostalgia lodges in your belly like a tapeworm, the bittersweet memory of a summer picnic at a lake somewhere with farting beery trombones and sun kissed children wading in the water. Most Americans, I think, and I imagine most people everywhere, regard the era in which they were children as a sort of Golden Age, a time when life was simple and good. Myself, I don't look back to my childhood with this kind of nostalgia, to a vanished Golden Age, because by the time I was born everything was already royally fucked up.

I look back instead to the nineteenth century.

It must have been a beautiful world, America in the nineteenth century. No television, no radio... People actually read books. Not trash, either. Dickens, Balzac, Herman Melville, Stephen Crane, the Bronte Sisters. And they wrote, ordinary people, they wrote beautiful letters. Complete sentences, rounded paragraphs. My great-grandfather, for example. I still have some of the letters he wrote to my great-grandmother back in 1899. Elegant letters, written in a stately hand, with all kinds of fancy loops and curlicues. And he was just an ordinary man, my great-grandfather, a workingman who helped to build the railroad.

A beautiful world, America in the nineteenth century—elegant, decorous, leisurely. But they killed you. They killed you in places like Shiloh and Cold Mountain and Gettysburg. Three thousand four hundred seventy-seven at Shiloh, for instance, in less than two days. And then there was child labor and slavery and genocide and tuberculosis.

My great-grandfather was a laborer, but my grandfather was a railroad brakeman, sixty years with the D&H. I'd sit on his lap when I was little, I remember, at the upstairs apartment on Watkins Avenue in Oneonta overlooking the tracks, and we'd look out at the yard together and watch the trains hooking up, and he'd pull his gold watch out of his vest pocket and squint at the dial, a gold pocket watch, and the bulging surface of the watch case was all scritch-scratched, etched with tiny soft lines, hundreds of tiny scratches, interlaced. And then he'd check the yard, my Grandpa, to see if the trains were running on time. In those days there was a rhythm to everything, there was an order to things, but now we're riding a runaway train that's carrying us all away to that final night where nothing is remembered and nothing matters.

I'M LIVING NOW WITH PONLOK. We have a trailer in the woods that we share with four other guys, Cambodians, plus Khamtai from Laos and Dionisio from Mexico City. Ponlok's overjoyed because he only has eight roommates. In Cambodia he had twenty-six. California is a paradise for Ponlok, for three reasons: he has a place to sleep, he gets something to eat, and nobody's shooting at him.

It was Dionisio who introduced us to the Birrieria, Mungy Nuncie and me. The Birrieria was a homey little place next to the bean field with goat horns mounted outside above the door. We'd get the birria tacos with onions and cilantro, and then we'd take a few tacos with us for breakfast. We were never short of money. Mungy Nuncie had her neurosurgeon and then there were the stoop laborers in the bean field. They were running trains on her. She'd give them a wholesale price. But when Dionisio learned that I was living under a bridge he got me the job at Dr. Sharpe's Source of Health, Big Bluto's sweatshop. He did me a favor, and I'm grateful, but sometimes I can't help wondering if I wasn't better off under the bridge. And I miss Mungy Nuncie.

There's that nostalgia again. It'll eat you up, nostalgia, if the hookworms don't.

Dionisio informs me that Big Bluto's looking at setting up sweatshops in Taiwan, Honduras and the Dominican Republic. He's thinking of joining Wal-Mart and Mattel in China, where sweatshop workers make eighty cents a day.

"Those fifty thousand people that was killed in the earthquake in China, they were the lucky ones," Dionisio told me. I had to agree with him. *Eighty fucking cents a day? Jesus fucking Christ, man.* A mercy killing, if there ever was one. They're better off dead, the lot of them. Damned fine gesture, too. It proves that we live in a human-hearted universe.

Big Bluto is king of the bushy eyebrows. Carmen insists they're toupees, eyebrow toupees. I didn't know there was such a thing. You run a couple of squirrel tails through a shit-shredder and paste them on his forehead, and there you have Big Bluto's eyebrows. Always there's a regular snowstorm of dandruff flakes falling down on his glasses, too. Big Bluto's eyebrows are infested with *Demodex Folliculorum*, eyebrow mites. They're eating his skin cells. He told me this himself the other day when he was watching me bottle the Coenzyme Q-10 caps. I guess he was looking for sympathy.

Carmen's in charge of the Clean Room. She's a very nice lady. *"No te preocupes,"* she told me the other day when I jammed the labeling machine. I don't think she suspects that I did it on purpose. We had a meeting today in the lunchroom, all the drudges who work in the Clean Room. Lucky for me I understand Spanish. Kiri—cute as a button—interpreted for the Cambodians. Carmen told us that tomorrow we're going to be bottling the Dr. Sharpe's Shakti Tonic, Big Bluto's biggest seller. Dr. Sharpe's Shakti Tonic—*"Calms the spirit, refreshes the senses, and nourishes the heart!"*—sells for a whopping forty-nine dollars a bottle. The label says it contains Ginko Biloba Leaf, Gotu Kola, Chinese Peony, Siberian Ginseng and Fleece Flower Root, but it's mostly grain alcohol. Dionisio and I are expecting to catch a pretty good buzz when we start bottling the stuff up tomorrow.

It was Dionisio who gave Big Bluto his name. "El Bluto Grande," he calls him.

Then there's Dr. Sharpe. He's our satguru, Dr. Sharpe, the Grand Tamale. Dr. Sharpe passed away in 1925. His picture hangs on the wall in the lunchroom, next to mug shots of the hookworms and the liver flukes, a man from the nineteenth century, a captain of industry, silvery hair, walrus mustache, kindly smile. Dr. Sharpe's Shakti Tonic was one of the biggies of the Patent Medicine Era, along with Lydia Pinkham's Vegetable Compound for Women, Dr. Kilmer's Swamp Root and Stanley's Snake Oil. And when Prohibition came along, Dr. Sharpe's Shakti Tonic took off like a rocket, mostly due to its hefty eighteen percent alcohol content. Today Big Bluto calls his Shakti Tonic "Instant Yoga." Why do all those asanas when you can just hook down a good slug of Dr. Sharpe's?

There's a gang of skateboarders, cheeky little runts, they zoom by the warehouse making a whole lot of clatter and noise. We see them, Dionisio and I, when we take out the trash. These little bastards are distinguished by their colossal arrogance. It's perfectly obvious that they hold us in utter contempt—because we're adults. They're certain, these lads, in their purity, in their hauteur, that they have all the answers. Everything is crystal clear to them, it's all black and white, everything cut and dried. They *know*. I was like that, too, sure I was, I mean when I was young. I had my own ideas; I was determined not to follow the crowd. *No compromise!* But now! My God, I'd do anything, say anything, agree to anything, for a mouthful of stale bread. Whatever the rest of them do, I'll do. If they say black is white and down is up, fine and dandy. If they march off a cliff, I'll be right behind them. I learned my lesson, by Jesus! *Know your place, do what you're told, kiss everybody's ass and say yes when you mean no.* That's the lesson I've learned in life.

A week has passed. Nostalgia got the better of me, so I went back to the bridge to see Mungy Nuncie. Things have escalated with the doctor. They've got the thing streamlined now. He sends a taxi for her, she goes to the office, and they get together between patients in one of the examination rooms. He takes his pecker out, she gives it a few silken strokes with her flippers, with those super-soft little turtle paws of hers, and he starts pumping sperm right away. When he's done squirting a nurse comes in, wipes his dick off with a Kleenex, tucks it back into his fly, and he scrubs for his next operation. Mungy Nuncie gets her hundred bucks, then the taxi driver takes her to Baskin Robbins and he has to wait while she gobbles up her banana split. But, a bit of sad news, the Birrieria is closed. The owner, the waitress and two cooks were killed in a driveby.

Today I was running the NC 400 encapsulating machine. You have to wear a mask. It looks like a WWI gasmask, with a canister and all. Inside the canister are paper filters and charcoal filters. But still the dust gets through. The worst is the wormwood, the dust you get when we encapsulate the wormwood powder. The turmeric is bad too. But the wormwood is poisonous. It's worse than mustard gas. And if you get sick? We don't have medical, no sick days and no vacation days. That's Big Bluto. Complain? Not unless you want to hit the bricks. There are hundreds of desperadoes camped out there in the tall weeds who'll snap up your job in a minute. Don't fuck with Hoppy!

But we did have a good laugh today, Dionisio and I. We learned through the grapevine that some of the monkeys in shipping boosted a whole shitload of Dr. Sharpe's Shakti Tonic and sold it on the street at five bucks a pop.

The time is coming, however, when I may have to put some distance between Dionisio and myself. I'm going to have to cut this joker loose, that's what I'm thinking. The other day we were over in the barrio on Sixth Street near Lafayette Park and Dionisio goes up to this ice cream vendor. I thought he was going to buy me an ice cream sandwich, but the guy opens up the top of his jingle cart and—guns. My man gave the ice cream guy some bills and pocketed a snub-nosed .38. Later on, when we were sitting in the park with a jug of Mona Lisa Tokay, he told me, "*First you get the money, then you get the power, and then you get the woman.*" He was serious, too. When Dionisio talks English he talks like Al Pacino. Bottom line is, he's bought into the dream, hook, line and sinker. But it's not for me. I'm not cut out for that sort of thing. If it's that hard to get the woman, I'd rather live under a bridge and jack off. But he's challenging me now, all the time. *Do I want to be a callejero all my life? Where's your cojones, man? You do what you gotta do to survive. If you want something, you take it.* I don't like being around Dionisio when he talks English. He's becoming a dangerous man.

Friday, that's payday. We decide to go to the Venus Bar to see a chick Dionisio's sweet on, Tina from Nicaragua. Dionisio's been having stomach trouble, so first we go to Grand Central Market, the China Cafe, for menudo, and then we tip a few. Dionisio goes to the toilet and when he comes back his face is pale and he's clutching his stomach. It's probably salmonella. Or it could be E. coli. Or the wormwood dust. Who knows?

"Maybe we shouldn't go to the bar."

"No, fuck it. I want you to meet Tina."

We walk from Third to Main. Whores lined up in front of La Herradura Restaurant next to the gutted Playland Dance Hall give us the eye. Open fires are flickering in the gutter in front of the Midnight Mission. We go over to Fifth Street and down, down into the medieval squalor that flourishes east of Los Angeles Street, smoking fires, hordes of ragged people settling into makeshift cardboard dwellings or squatting on sidewalks choked with rotting garbage and swigging from bottles of wine. I feel a surge of adrenaline. I've got less than six dollars on me, and no jewelry, but I'm afraid they'll kill me for my shoes.

"What's the matter, man? You escared?"

"Yes."

"Bullshit." He pulls up his shirt and shows me his .38 Special.

"Look, I'm going back, *ese*," I tell him.

"No! *No te dejas.* Keep going. Just one more block. Keep your head down. Don't look at anybody."

Finally, the Venus Bar, a scorpion's nest on Central Avenue, near the big oriental fish market. This is the place, and I'm hoping, for Dionisio's sake, that Tina's here. Standing at the bar, blinking our eyes like night-flying bats, we order drinks, a Cuba Libre for Dionisio, a Carta Blanca for me. Tina's sitting by herself at a table with her back to us. A satiny red dress cut low in the back, her hair up, slim, trim, nice solid ass. Dionisio has the bartender take her a Seven and Seven. *Slick.*

"Just like Carlito at *El Paraisio*," Dionisio mutters under his breath. Tina whirls and smiles, sloshing her drink. Dionisio, with his elbow resting on the bar, raises his glass and gives her a broad, careless grin, the Carlito smile. Tina comes over. Her teeth are dazzling in the soft light.

After a moment, Tina's friend, Lola from Sinaloa, joins us. We sit in a booth. Dionisio orders more drinks, and Dionisio and Tina dance. Then Lola and I dance. I feel like a scarecrow tossed on a breeze, my arms and legs swaying and snapping disjointedly, propelled by flashes of lightning. Lola is bouncy, talkative, lively. She tells me in Spanish that Tina and Dionisio have been talking about getting married.

"*No me digas!*"

"Well, when are *you* getting married?" she asks in English.

"When you tell me *si*," I answer.

"You are *crasy*," she says, laughing. "I am too much older for you. You have not seen my face in the light."

When the music stops she gets a photo out of her purse, her boy, Luis, a Lance Corporal at Camp Pendleton. The next number begins. "*Bailamos?*" I venture, and lovely Lola's in my arms again. Glancing over her shoulder through the powder-swirl of music I see Dionisio sitting in the booth, drumming his fingers, gazing down at his drink. Things aren't going well, I gather. It's the stomach business, plus Tina's off dancing with some *cholo*. Leti gazes up at me like a guppy, her mouth open.

"You want me—to marry—with you? *No seas tonto.* You have not seen my face in the light."

Back at the booth, Dionisio is smiling grimly, patting his gun. The dancers are swaying, the jukebox pulses like a living heart spurting thick ropes of blood. I gaze into Dionisio's shiny black eyes, the Carlito eyes, festering with ambition and greed.

"This is bullshit! Did you see the way that Tina cunt slipped away from me? Did you see that *maricon* she was dancing with? I'll blow that motherfucker away, man!"

A fat woman in a pink dress has taken off her shoe and she's scratching her back with the spike heel while a blissful smile spreads across her face.

Dionisio leans across the table. "I think I'm gonna puke again. Wait for me, okay?"

"Yeah, yeah, yeah."

Dionisio goes to the toilet and I'm left with Lola, lovely Lola from Sinaloa. We talk, naturally enough, about Dionisio.

"*Es muy delicado, este,*" I tell her.

"He's *quir?*"

"No, it's his stomach. *Estómago. Me entiendes?*"

"Ah! *Si, su estómago.* I onder-estand. He no likey fuck?"

Tina returns to the booth and then Dionisio returns. The kissy, dovey, romancy music flows on. Couples paw one another in the booths. The woman in the pink dress is dancing with a sailor. The *maricon* has split. He must have realized that Dionisio is packing. So everything's okay now. Dionisio is hugging Tina; he's squeezing her titties. He slips me a stage wink along with the careless Carlito grin. *Tranquilo!* I kiss Lola's guppy mouth again and again.

"So, you want to marry with me?" she murmurs, unbuttoning my shirt. "*Ten cuidado, guero. You have not seen my face in the light...*"

3

SOMETHING'S ROTTEN IN DENMARK," Big Bluto announced at the company meeting today. At first I thought he was talking about the ten cases of Dr. Sharpe's Shakti Tonic that the Colombian guys boosted, but it turned out he was talking about a rat—the four-legged kind. Big Bluto put out rattraps in all the corners and under the counters in the lunchroom, and now it appears that a rat got caught in one of the traps and dragged the trap through a hole in the wall, and he's rotting inside the wall. The stink is fierce, but I have to laugh, because Big Bluto has to put up with it, same as the rest of us. I mean, we all breathe the same air. The difference is, we're used to foul odors and he isn't.

This rotten in Denmark bit was Big Bluto's way of kissing up to us. He thought he was being cute. But most of the workers have never heard of Hamlet, Prince of Denmark. They don't have Shakespeare Festivals in the shantytowns of Phnom Penh.

Things were different in Shakespeare's time. War, slavery, child labor: sure. That's the world. But you could drink the water. You could breathe the air. Bluto's world is dying. The signs are everywhere. The super bugs are with us now: Golden staph, VRE, enterococcus; lean, furious mosquitoes that eat DDT for breakfast, amoebas that eat your eyes. The big diseases are coming back: cholera, tuberculosis, diphtheria. They've been sharpening their incisors in the dark, rehearsing their lines just offstage. And now they're ready to pounce. It's not only Denmark that's rotting away like a diseased rat. The stink is everywhere. The Bluto World is dunged under, played out. Only an influx of barbarian sperm can save it now. That's the only hope. The wombs of the Bluto women are crying for it.

Big Bluto, with his Swiss bank accounts, connected all the way up to the Texas oil families and the Saudi princes, is nervous as hell. The richer he gets, the more he worries. Because what he's doing, with all his money and his connections, is reserving himself a stateroom on the Titanic. The ship is going down. And he knows it. He won't admit it, even to himself, but he knows it. The Bluto World is jacked. The whole stinking edifice is crumbling, shaking off its foundations, rotting away like a termite hill. Rats are gnawing the taproots; carpet beetles are tunneling under the wallpaper. But a new world is already in the making. The barbarians appear at the gates of the city, their eyes sizzling with vitamins, their loins freighted with erotic dynamite. A silvery trumpet sounds somewhere, and conquered and conquerors gaze at each other like moist flowers opening in the light of a new and dazzling sun.

IF YOU SPEND MUCH TIME IN THE STREET you'll find that a lot of your homeless will have their own signature stench. Crazy Kermit, for example: Crazy Kermit was with us for a few days under the bridge. Before he joined us he used to sleep in a grease pit. So there was the stink of axle grease plus the smell of stale sweat. Not just stale sweat, but stale on top of stale on top of stale. *Fermented* sweat. And then, of course, every once in a while Crazy Kermit would load his pants. That was Crazy Kermit's signature stench—axle grease, fermented sweat and human shit. He wasn't a bad egg aside from the stink. We'd make sure he got breakfast every morning, the birria tacos. Then we'd send him out into the world and he'd spend the day sitting on a bus bench barking like a dog.

We had another guy with us for a while, Ike or Mike. He didn't go out at all. He was shattered, shell-shocked. Post-traumatic stress syndrome. He'd crouch under the bridge, shaking like a leaf, his clenched hands shiny with ground-in dirt. Never ate breakfast. Mungy Nuncie would give me some money and I'd go to a little bodega and bring back his four forty-ounce King Cobras for the day. "If it don't sting, it ain't the King," he'd say. Those were the only words I ever heard him utter, so I never knew exactly what happened to him in the war. He'd try to talk sometimes, but it was mostly gibberish that came out of his mouth. As nearly as I could figure, it wasn't what they did to *him*, it was what he had to do to *them*. He lost his humanity over there, and he wasn't going to be getting it back any time soon, at least not crouching under a bridge pounding forty-ounce King Cobras.

A month has gone by. Quality Control found rat hairs in the Pau d'Arco Powder. The Pau d'Arco Powder is supposedly imported from the Brazilian rainforest, but most likely it's just ground up eucalyptus bark and cockroach bodies. Big Bluto steps on it too, with baby laxative, just like the coke dealers.

Things came to a boil with Dionisio, my Tony Montana. Two weeks ago at the trailer he was strapped and coked up to beat the band. He's going to take down a liquor store near Lafayette Park and he wants me to come along. Not a chance, I tell him. And where's he getting the money for the toot, I wonder? I don't want to know.

You're headed down the wrong path, Chico.

Don't call me Chico. What's the matter with you? Where's your cojones, man? You ain't never gonna do nothing. You know what you are, *ese*? You're just a Fifth Street wino!

I tell him in Spanish: "That guy behind the counter is just a poor son of a bitch working for poverty wages. I walk in there with a gun, and supposing he's strapped and he throws down on me, and I punch his ticket for him. Then I've killed one of my own. You understand? I can't do that. I won't."

I haven't seen Dionisio since that night. I've prayed that he didn't get blown away, or pinched and deported, but I'm relieved too. He was starting to push the envelope. He was becoming a cowboy.

JIMMY D WAS ANOTHER ONE like Dionisio who bought into the Carlito dream, the Goodfellas dream. That's why he called himself Jimmy D instead of Jimmy D'Angelo. But I didn't have to worry about Jimmy D knocking over a liquor store. He never would have done something like that. Jimmy D was an ineffectual dreamer, like me.

Here we are standing on Broadway, in front of the Million Dollar Theater, Jimmy D in his buckskin jacket with the flowing fringe and a turquoise bolo tie, his ten-gallon hat, the long wavy gray hair, and his persimmon-sour expression. He scuffs the heel of his cowboy boot on the pavement, as if he's trying to drive in a loose nail, then pops his fingers, like he's just remembered something: "Did you see how that barmaid looked at us? Like we was a couple of Fifth Street winos! Come on, let's go to Maria's. Maybe we can shake a couple of cunts loose. I never had this goddamn trouble in New York. The goddamn women in this fucking country think because they got a crack between their legs they fucking own the world. Boy, I'd like to take some of these bitches over to the Orient where life ain't worth three cents."

That's the way we usually started out our evenings. Then he'd tell me for the millionth time about the night he saw Sinatra at Jilly's. Apparently it was the landmark event of his life: '*I feel sorry for people who don't drink*,' Old Blue

Eyes told me. '*When they wake up in the morning, that's as good as they're going to feel all day.*' Later on there was that concert in Vegas. I called him up. 'Frank,' I says, 'I'd like to make that concert,' I says. 'Jimmy D,' he says, 'no problem. I'm sending you the tickets, baby.' That's what he said to me, man! *Frank Sinatra!*"

Jimmy D had three main topics of conversation: Frank Sinatra, "the goddamn women in this fucking country", and his stomach problems. The stomach business, with Jimmy D, wasn't salmonella. It was shrapnel. Jimmy D did thirty years in the Army. We'd go to Cole's for a few beers when his pension check came in. Another place we frequented was the China Cafe in Grand Central Market. We'd tip a few and then we'd go to Maria's for the fish tacos, or sometimes the *siete mares*, a fish soup with everything in it, shrimps, crab, lobster claws, fish chunks and scallops. Get it down and you're set for the day, maybe even for a week.

We used to go to LaMonica's, too, a pizza dive on Sixth, for New York style pizza, or sometimes just for beers and to reminisce. They had a 'Fulton Fish Market' sign tacked up on the wall. Jimmy D and I had both been to the Chinese New Year celebrations on Mulberry Street, and the Italian street fairs, and we'd bought bread at Zampieri's Bakery on Sullivan Street, near Saint Anthony's Cathedral. Once we demolished the pizza the rest of the interlude was devoted to Jimmy D's getting it out—his despair, his hopelessness, his defeat.

"I thought when we came back from Nam that there'd be something. I don't know, some sort of recognition. They could have fucking done something."

"Like what?"

"I don't know, man. Like they could have given us… They could have given us a parade."

A parade? Sorry, Jimmy D. The parades are only for the generals. Do you mean to tell me you haven't learned that by now?

One night we went to see Jasmine at Dreamland. But

first we had to get tanked up. Jasmine was one of those girls from Minnesota who come to LA to make movies. She'd worked at LaMonica's early on. Then she got the dime-a-dance job. Her dream, besides making movies, was to get enough money for piano lessons. Jimmy D was sweet on Jasmine, and so was I.

We go to Maria's. I choose the tacos de pollo, refritos, rice, and a Carta Blanca to wash it down. I feel a momentary surge of importance as I dictate my order to the pudgy waitress sweating in her white ruffled blouse. Jimmy D leans back in the booth and hoists his beer. "Here's to ya, bro!" He's at his best now; it's early in the evening and the Sinatra fantasy seems real. I'm feeling good too. I enjoy Jimmy D's company when he's in this mood. He doesn't require as much attentiveness as when he's pouring his misery out, bleeding all over me from South Broadway to Bonnie Brae Street.

After the meal we hit the toilet so Jimmy D can comb his hair in the mirror. He takes off the sombrero and sculpts his elaborate pompadour, then wipes off the comb with a piece of toilet paper.

"Fuckin' cheap terlit paper they got in these jernts. Come on, bro, let's blow this pop-stand."

Vain as a rooster, he replaces the sombrero. He's all puffed up like some movie gangster.

We go to a dive on Sixth. The alcohol is starting to do a job on Jimmy D's guts.

"*Perforated*, that's what they are. My goddamn guts are riddled like a Swiss cheese. The goddamn stuff...is dripping through. It burns like poison!" He grabs his drink and gags half of it down, then doubles over, gasping and clutching his belly. "Jesus Christ," he whispers, "You can't fucking win!"

'Perforated' is one of Jimmy D's favorite words. He's proud of the stockpile of scientific words he's picked up from reading his medical reports in the drafty corridors of veterans' hospitals and free clinics. He realizes, of course, that since his duodenum is perforated, he shouldn't be drinking. But—

"I'm still a fuckin' human being, ain't I?"

A moment later: "Did you ever take a breath and it felt like your lungs wasn't drawing nothing but water? Like the goddamn juice was spritzin' around inside you, like your ribs was a birdcage squeezing shit through an accordion? You think I wanted them medics cutting on me? You think I *requested* it? Boy, I'd like to get my hands on the cocksucker that used a knife on me at that General Beaumont Hospital in Texas. They cut my fucking guts out, man. You know what I'd do? You know what I'd do if I got my hands on those bastards? I'd send them all over to the Orient where life ain't worth three cents!"

Thanks to these conversations of ours I know Jimmy D's visceral landscape as well as I know the streets of LA—the waffle-weave terrain, the bottom lands and the badlands, the alkali flats pocked with bomb craters, the tortured blowpipes, the wrecked tubing and the steaming geysers. I know the dead-end gullies and the crazy ravines choked with automobile graveyards and poisoned wells, and I know the shallow bitter seas, the deserted cities, the haunted streets festering with jungle rot, the hissing valves and galvanized elbows that piss battery acid and gangrene like a broken accordion. The story of Jimmy D's perforated duodenum is a symphony that repeats itself endlessly in my mind, a New World Symphony punched out on a garbage can lid with a nine-inch stiletto.

We make it to the Dreamland Dance Hall. Good old Dreamland! It's a hole in the wall, sure, old and rundown, but a great place for buying affection. We sit at a table, blinking our eyes to get them used to the darkness. They don't serve alcohol at Dreamland. But Jimmy D is prepared. He takes a flat bottle out of his cowboy boot and sweetens our Cokes with Kentucky Deluxe. But things go off on a bum tangent. Jasmine's in a clinch with some mouth-breather and there's a fire raging in Jimmy D's guts.

He leans across the table and gazes at me earnestly.

"I puked up some blood back at that jernt on Broadway. You know?"

"Yeah, yeah."

"You spend thirty-two months rotting your guts in the General Beaumont Hospital in Texas and what the fuck do you get? A bunch of cheap-ass medals that ain't worth a Kennedy half dollar at the hock shop." He raises his glass, his brown eyes simmering with rage. "*Fuck you, Texas!* If Texas was a pay toilet, I wouldn't pay a nickel to shit on Texas."

What happened next happened fast. Jimmy D upchucked on the table. It wasn't just the *tacos de pollo* and the refried beans. There was blood in it—a lot of blood. And Jimmy D, pale as a ghost, was clutching his guts. I ran to the counter and called 911. The medics appeared minutes later. Everything stopped: the music, the dancing. The medics hustled Jimmy D out and that was it. I asked if I could ride along but they couldn't permit it. Then Jasmine got loose from the yayhoo she'd been wrestling with and came over to the table. We talked for a few minutes, but rules are rules at the Dreamland Dance Hall and I only had enough money in my pocket to dance with her for seven minutes, so I said good night and promised I'd look in on Jimmy D and get back to her.

Then came a period when I didn't see Jimmy D for a while. It was as if he'd dropped off the edge of the world. When I finally met up with him at Grand Central Market he'd just come from the handout line at St. Vincent de Paul's. They'd raised the rent at the Rosslyn and he'd moved from the Rosslyn to the Hotel Cecil without telling anyone. Then some street duchess ripped him off, his whole pension check. He couldn't pay his rent at the Hotel Cecil. He'd spent a month in the street, making the rounds of the missions, staying up all night in coin laundries, or sometimes sleeping in Lafayette Park. We had a few beers at the China Café, and then the fish tacos at Maria's. I was camping with a friend at the time. We caught a bus to Hollywood.

While Jimmy D's in the shower I find a bottle of Wild Irish Rose in the fridge, and Jimmy D and I pass the bottle back and forth and suddenly things are the way they used to be.

"I want to get out of this city," he said. "I want to go up to Vermont, or Alaska, and catch fish through a hole in the ice. Did you ever look into a fish's eyes? They don't go through all the fucking bullshit we have to grapple with twenty-four hours a day. They don't have to think because they don't have a mind. They don't worry about anything. They just live and they die, and there's a lot to be said for that.

"Yeah, I'd like to go up to the Klondike. Be a squaw man. You know? I want one that's nice and oily. A big oily Madonna with the bacon between her legs. You know the kind I'm talking about. I don't care how big she is, as long as she's got the bacon between her legs. A gal like that'll keep you warm at night. Jesus, can you picture it, how it'd be, when she wraps her legs around you? I don't want to watch myself in the mirror anymore. I just want to pretend it's a fucking Forties movie and I'm Bogart and she's Little Miss Wonderful on the skids. I want everything to be like it was. I just want to close my eyes and dream it. Vermont or Maine or the Klondike. Get myself an Indian squaw, a big oily Indian squaw who'll wrap her legs around me and wash everything away. We'll crawl under the buffalo hides and she'll wrap her legs around me, and it'll be dark, dark, and I can see whatever I want to see. And we'll wash it away. We'll wash it all away..."

In the months that followed, Jimmy D moved from the Hotel Cecil to the Barclay and then to the Madison near 7th and San Julian. He was descending farther and farther into the bowels of the city. He was drinking hard. Whenever I ran into him I pressed a few dollars into his hands if I had it. Often I wasn't sure if he recognized me or not. One afternoon I saw him sitting in the nightmare alley behind the Rosslyn Hotel, Harlem Place. His buckskin jacket was ragged and filthy, and he'd lost his sombrero. He'd been coughing up blood, and there was bright red blood on his handkerchief.

"I was always sorry I couldn't make it to Frank's funeral," he said. "Jack Nicholson was there, Dom DeLuise, Tony Danza. They played 'Put Your Dreams Away,' man. 'Put Your Dreams Away.' That's a fuckin' classic…"

I gave him three dollars and then I left, at his request, to buy a bottle of Night Train. Five minutes later, when I got back to Harlem Place, he was gone. I guess he was embarrassed to have me see him in such a dragged-out condition. I never saw Jimmy D again. I like to think that he made it to Jilly's, but it's more probable that he descended into the Dante's Inferno that lies east of Los Angeles Street in the vicinity of Fifth, where inevitably, the jaws of the city gulped him down.

4

THE SHIT HAS HIT THE FAN AT THE SWEATSHOP. Big Bluto found out about the ten cases of Dr. Sharpe's Shakti Tonic. He fired the Colombians and ratted them out to La Migra. He installed security gates, cameras—the works. It's him versus us now. The lines are drawn. The new guys in Shipping are illegals from Mogadishu, obviously dangerous men. The big one with the ring through his nose is called Tariq. What is Big Bluto thinking? Obviously, he intends to use these desperadoes as muscle, to keep the rest of us in line.

Don't fuck with Hoppy!

He's going to get his revenge, too. This time it's poor little Kiri who'll have to pay the price. She's going to have to suck Bluto's dick. If she refuses he'll report her to immigration and she'll be back in the sweatshop in Phnom Penh with the one hundred- degree heat and the razor wire, and she'll have to suck that guy's dick. She's reconciled to her fate. I can see it in her face. He'll call her into his office sometime today. The girls in the Clean Room are furious. But there's nothing they can do. They've all been down the same road. It comes with the territory. Carmen has had Bluto's cock in her mouth God knows how many times. And poor little Ana from

Guatemala: so innocent, so devout! She can't be more than seventeen. Bluto likes them young. *Old enough to bleed, old enough to butcher.* He plucked her out of the lunchroom just the other day. One minute she was unwrapping her quesadilla and saying grace, and the next minute she was on her knees behind some boxes in the warehouse with Big Bluto's cock halfway down her throat.

Later. Big Bluto's feeling jolly after a good sperm-sucking. Who wouldn't? He scoots across the room in his office chair, clicking his calculator, crunching the numbers. Carmen's been talking about putting rat poison in his coffee. Here's hoping she gets a chance to sprinkle the magic dust! We'd all like to see Big Bluto croak. But it's not going to be so easy. He's got Tariq with him now, always at his side. Tariq stands there with his arms folded, glaring at us like a big evil genie. He's out of the bottle, and he's as nasty a piece of work as you'll ever come across.

Monday. The Grand Dragon came out of his oval office this morning with the Dr. Sharpe parasite book under his arm and gave us another lecture. Those of us who understand English were laughing up our sleeves. *We're* the parasites, aren't we? We're the hookworms, the tapeworms, the liver flukes and the pinworms. We're everywhere now, there's no escaping us. March us off to war, starve us out, banish us to the streets, a million more spring up. We're the microbes that live deep in the bedrock, in the heart of a diamond, below the polar ice, in the center of a volcano, on Jupiter's moons. We're the weevils in the flour, the rats in the cheese; we're the lice that burrow under Big Bluto's skin. We're the horror that's festering in his soul. We're renegade cells in the Body of Bluto.

Big Bluto has an ulcer in his stomach the size of a golf ball. It's true. Our CEO can't even eat a decent meal. He can't order lobster or steak at a restaurant, either. Baby food: that's what he eats. *Junior* Foods. I know because he eats with us, nearly every day. This is to show us his compassion, his willingness to walk the sod with the unwanted. It's democracy in action. Carmen places Big Bluto's specially prepared plate in front of him, colorful dollops of baby food garnished with parsley and lemon wedges. Usually it's Junior Vegetables: carrots and green beans. Or Junior Chicken and Vegetables. Then she brings his mango lassi. For dessert he usually has the strained peaches.

IT'S EXCRUCIATING BEING A NOTHING, but there are advantages to it. You're free, in a way. Take me, for example. Nobody expects anything of me. They know better. But all that changed when I met Pablito. He was a crazy Catholic kid, the archetypal immigrant; passionate, hopeful, single minded, intent on making a new life in America for himself and his family. On his first try he'd crossed the Sonoran desert with his wife and child. He got a job shoveling guts in a slaughterhouse in Fresno, but after a month he was nabbed and deported. His wife and baby remained behind. On the second try he came through the Nogales Wash, a sewer pipe that connects Nogales, Sonora with Nogales, Arizona. Now he was on a mission to find his wife and child. He'd gotten word that they were living in a migrant labor camp in McGonigle Canyon, near San Diego. His one objective was to join them, but first he had to get some money. He didn't want to show up empty handed.

Pablito was very religious, like little Ana from Guatemala. He prayed to the Virgin of Guadalupe every day. He never used words like *pinche* or *puto*, and not even *cabrón*. He had very little English, but he knew all the words to the Sinatra song, "New York, New York," and he was always singing it.

"Start spreading the news, I'm leaving today…"

I bought into Pablito's story. I liked the guy; I admired him. I got involved. I felt a sense of civic responsibility.

Me! I couldn't believe it. But my people came here from Ireland and Germany, didn't they? I mean when you go way back? I guess you could even say I felt patriotic. What ever happened to *give me your tired, your poor?* If Lady Liberty had dropped the torch, wasn't it my job to pick it up? Pablito was a brave kid, and I had to help him. So I ended up borrowing Bobbo's van and driving Pablito to McGonigle Canyon. But that came later...

Pablito was bright and enterprising, a willing worker. He and I were assigned to mixing the Coenzyme Q-10 powder, "the Q," under Big Bluto's watchful eye. Bluto steps on the Q with Vitamin B-2 powder. You can't use baby laxative with the Q because it's the wrong color. The B-2 is the right color, bright yellow, and it's dirt-cheap. The Q goes for ten thousand dollars a kilo, wholesale. Bluto would buy ten keys at a time, and then we'd add the B-2 powder. You mix in the B-2 at a ratio of 1:4, and you'd never tell the difference just looking at it, but when you get done Bluto has picked up two and a half keys or twenty-five g's.

The batch mixer, made in Germany, must have cost a fortune. It sounded like an F 86 winding up. We'd feed both kinds of powder into the hopper, or sometimes we'd use a suction wand. It was fascinating to imagine what was going on inside. There was a big worm gear that fed the powder into an array of paddles and multiple air jets that tumbled and mixed everything up. We'd run it twice, just to make sure. This job was high tech, and it bumped up our status with the cuties in the Clean Room when they saw us sporting our bug-like respirator masks. The mixer was in a room by itself. Bluto watched every move we made through a little square window, like the window the priest looks through when you're strapped into the electric chair.

THE END CAME SUDDENLY, I mean at the sweatshop. A raid. La Migra. They came in with guns and megaphones, just like the movies. *Manos arriba, motherfuckers!* They got the Somalians, Tariq, everybody, thirty-five illegals all told. It was a debacle. Big Bluto and I were the only American citizens, except for a sweet fat lady named La Tanya who'd worked in billing for years. There was also an old Mexican guy with a blue Dodge pickup truck who collected pallets and sold them. He just happened to be driving by and they nailed him too. It was devastating, losing my friends and my job, but I was happy to see Bluto go down. I also knew of course that he'd buy his way out of it, pay off the cops, pay off the judge, and the rest of it. The Big Blutos of the world always come out smelling sweet.

I RAN INTO JACK AGAIN. He had his arm all the way down a trashcan in front of a yoga studio on Hollywood Boulevard. He looked up at me and flashed a gap-toothed grin. "Hi bro!" Then he came up with the prize he'd been digging for: a tall paper cup with a straw still sticking out of the top.

"Smoothie," he said, smacking his lips. "Pineapple. Still cold. Want some?"

"I'll pass, Jack."

We took a stroll down Halloween Boulevard and Jack filled me in on what had been happening in his so-called life. He'd been to every piano bar in LA looking for Tony, but the Big Guy was nowhere to be found. He'd been to the missions, too, and the shelters, and he'd visited any number of the charming cardboard villages that have sprung up like diseased mushrooms here and there in the streets of LA.

"I don't know," Jack declared. "Maybe he caught a freight. Maybe he went back to New York, that piano bar on Houston. They said he could work anytime he wanted. But I don't like to think of Tony riding the rails by himself."

"Jesus! Why did you guys come out here in the first

place if Tony already had a gig in New York? It doesn't make sense. And what do you mean about Tony not traveling alone? Tony's a big guy. He's built like a brick shithouse."

"Yeah, but he's…I don't know…he's *naïve*. And he's deaf. I told you that. He don't speak the language. And he's drunk. He's real drunk. He's drunk on his ass, every minute of the day. And why did we come to California? I don't know why. The Golden Land, I guess. I don't know. We were drunk. Why does it have to make sense? Does anything make sense? The world's upside down, man. Say, you want to get on a wine?"

We wandered around some more and drank some wine. I had some money on me. We ran into Crazy Kermit from the bridge, too. He was sitting on a bus bench babbling, making intricate gestures with his hands, as if he were conducting an invisible orchestra. I went up to him and gave him a dollar. He didn't recognize me, but that was okay because Crazy Kermit doesn't recognize anybody.

Jack told me about the place where he was staying in Boyle Heights, a condemned building. I'd been camping out with the Lump, and then when that fell apart I moved in with Kenji, but I was scared with the drugs and all. We'd leave Uncle Barney's and Kenji would be higher than a hawk and leaning out the window talking a blue streak to people in other cars and he'd have the crank on him, too. Supposing we got pulled over for a brake light or something and… Well, I don't even want to think about the rest of it.

The Lump was a funny duck. A big guy, six feet four, but he lived in a perpetual twilight. Valium, Seconal, Prozac, I'm not sure what they gave him at the nuthouse, but he was heavily sedated. Then, too, he was constantly pounding the wine, and the hard stuff like Crown Royal and Absolut Vodka.

The Lump had a studio apartment in Hollywood. You

could see the famous Hollywood sign from the window. I'd walk in and he'd smile. No greeting, but his mild blue eyes would twinkle faintly, like distant stars. He'd sit there on his mattress, packing his bong, humming to himself. Once in a while he'd send out for a pizza. He didn't seem to care about eating. Money wasn't a problem. His parents lived in Rancho Santa Fe. They were paying him to stay away, the apartment and a monthly stipend.

I met the Lump at Rite Aid. He'd just boosted a bottle of Crown Royal. He knew I made him so when we both got outside he offered me a drink. I wouldn't have said anything, of course. He was agoraphobic, the Lump. He carried a tennis racket with him for protection whenever he ventured out, which was seldom. About the only place he ever went was Rite Aid for Crown Royal or Absolut Vodka. He'd stash the tennis racket in the bushes when he went inside.

The Lump was a consummate shoplifter. I used to go along. It was a pleasure to watch him work. He knew everyone at Rite Aid and the counter girls were nuts about him. He was tall and handsome, and he had a superficial air of assurance and savoir-faire. You'd never think, just looking at him, that he was a drug addict and insane. One time I saw him boost three bottles of Crown Royal. He simply picked up the bottles and walked out with them, he was that good.

Occasionally a hunchback in blackened rags would come to the door of the apartment. This was Quasimodo, Quazi for short. He lived in a cardboard box out by the dumpster. He'd knock at the door, very humble and apologetic. *"Could I have the resin from your pipe?"* The Lump would hand him the pipe and Quazi would scrape out half a teaspoon of ghetto hash. He'd give Quazi a slice of pizza, too, and Quazi would grin delightedly. His little stubby teeth were orange and wiggly. Then he'd scuttle away, crablike, and we wouldn't see him for a day or so. The neighbors used to put food out for Quazi, in a metal dog dish. He'd do a little monkey dance, too, up around Grumman's Chinese, holding out his cap for coins. The tourists loved him. Once I looked out the window and I saw Quazi fussing with a can of Sterno. I thought he was going to make Pink Lady, but later I peeked out and he was using the Sterno to roast a rat he'd somehow managed to catch.

The Lump's place was a regular magnet. Beggars and dope freaks clustered outside, like penitents around a cathedral, especially at the end of the month when the Lump's SSI check came in. There'd been a girl in the picture at one point. Francine. He'd met her at a sober living house. Nobody knew much about her. She was in the women's prison at Las Colinas. Then there was the lady upstairs, Madam Butterfly. She had a crush on him, but she was a lot older. She'd come to the door wanting to borrow a cup of sugar. We called her Madam Butterfly because of the way her hands fluttered. She had Parkinson's Disease.

The Lump had so many prescriptions you couldn't shake a stick at them. Seconal, Neurotonin, Prozac, Valium, Percodan—"Perks"—Vicodin, of course, and then he got a prescription for OxyCotin—"Oxies". That brought half the junkies in Hollywood to his door. They were coming out of the woodwork.

The Lump liked to mix the pills up to see what they'd do. He'd take a handful, uppers and downers, and swallow them with Crown Royal. No wonder he eventually od'd. I never knew whether it was deliberate or not. He was in there for a week before they found the body. It was the lady upstairs, Madam Butterfly. The stink got to her, so she called the cops. Then the parents showed up, the father with a crisp white mustache, polo shirt and a camel hair sport coat, and the mother in a navy blue cardigan with tiny pearl buttons. They didn't seem to be all that broken up over their son's death. They were probably glad to be rid of him.

Jack and I got on a bus for Boyle Heights.

"Condemned building, huh? Sounds good."

"Yeah, bro. Wait till you see it."

The abandoned building was great. It was one of several leering tenements squatting at the end of a dead end street. Beyond a rusty chain link fence, puddles of black water, slag heaps and piles of wrecked machinery oozed a putrid crude oil stench while stunted trees poked their broken arms at a yellow sky.

We went inside. A few scarecrows cowered here and there in corners, snoozing or swilling wine, but there was plenty of room. Unfortunately, there was a spot of bother, as they say. Jack hadn't told me the whole story.

"We can't hang out here," Jack said. "The fuckin' heat. They raid the place every night. High visibility."

We went back outside. I was pissed. "Then why the fuck did you bring me all the way out here, Jack?" I felt like letting the air out of him.

"Underneath," Jack declared brightly. He was obviously feeling very proud of himself. "Underneath the building, man. I got myself an underground hooch. Come on."

We walked around to the side of the building. I just felt like getting the hell out of there. But on the other hand I was curious. Plus night was coming on. It was a long way back to Kenji's place, and I had to sleep somewhere.

"You gotta take a dump or anything? You can go over there in those bushes." He pulled some napkins out of his pocket. Jack's pockets were always stuffed with napkins, packets of sugar and catsup, plastic forks and spoons, what have you. "Once we get under there, you know, it's not a good idea for us to be going in and out."

We get down on our knees and Jack pulls a bundle dried up weeds aside. There's a hole in some chicken wire big enough for a man to crawl through. I feel a cool breeze and there's a damp earth smell that's curiously inviting.

Jack pats his stomach and belches. "Ah! A pineapple burp. That smoothie, you know? It was almost full, man.

Still cold. Those fuckin' cuties at the yoga studio got money up the ass. They'll take a couple sips and toss it in the trash. I go by there all the time. Best pickings in town! They got raspberry, blueberry, strawberry, pineapple—the whole shmegeggi. Well, you ready?"

We crawl inside and Jack carefully covers the opening with the bunch of dry weeds. I blink my eyes to get them used to the darkness. I see a big hollowed-out area, like a shallow grave, Jack's bedroll, some clothes, a wine jug and a shovel with half of the handle cut off.

"Welcome to the Black Hole of Calcutta! We're plenty safe under here. But the rats'll be along tonight, after it gets dark. They're your Norwegian rats. The big ones. Size of fox terriers, some of them. Those things'll bite your pecker off while you're asleep. Think I'm kidding? It happens, man. *Snip, snip!* They got teeth like razors. They're attracted to crotch rot, too. And gangrene. They like that cheesy smell. So if you haven't taken a bath in a while, you're fuckin' rat bait!"

Jack was putting me on, I knew. It was his way. The wine was Gallo zinfandel, dry as dust, but surprisingly good, and it certainly did the trick. It never hurts to blur the edges a bit.

Jack was just getting wound up.

"Yeah, I ran into some of those little bastards up in Seattle. I was sleeping in this dumpster. There was a bunch of cardboard in that sucker, and you could hear their claws scraping on that smooth cardboard—the rats, I mean—*scritch, scritch, scritch*—all fucking night. *Scritch, scritch, scritch!* And I couldn't climb out of the dumpster. The place was alive with cops. But we're okay under here. There's something safe about the smell of dirt. You were in the Army, weren't you? I mean, you look like the type. Remember your entrenching tool? How it folds up? You remember digging in? I always felt safe when I was dug in. I loved my entrenching tool. The smell of fresh dirt, you know? That fresh earth smell. Then along comes the

Colonel of the Urinal. Remember? *'You call this a foxhole, soldier? Stand up straight when I talk to you!'* Turkey-ass motherfuckers."

We were sitting in the dirt. I was resting my back against a piling. The floor of the building was a foot or so above our heads. You could crouch but you couldn't stand up. I asked Jack where a guy might be able to take a leak.

"Right over there," he said proudly, pointing at a hole in the ground some distance away. "I dug a little trench, too. That's my toilet. You can piss in it, but if you have to do the other thing you gotta go outside."

An hour or so went by. We heard some thumping topside. Jack said it was probably the cops, rousting everybody out. We polished off the whole jug of Gallo zinf. Jack had an extra blanket for me.

"I met a man and his wife in a homeless shelter," Jack said softly as we settled in. "The woman told me that rats gnawed their baby's feet off. I don't know if it was true or not. 'And then they ate her little shoes,' she told me. Somehow that made me sad as hell, that detail, you know? *They ate her little shoes!* It's crazy the things you remember. Like the smell of dirt, that fresh earth smell. You smell it in springtime when the snow's melting and muddy water's running in the gutters. I'd be walking to school and I'd have my lunch, the peanut butter and jelly sandwiches my mother made for me, and I never thought back then that someday I'd be homeless and hiding in a dumpster with Norwegian fucking rats—*scritch, scritch, scritch*—gnawing at my pecker and balls while I'm trying to sleep. But the whole world is crumbling now. They're running out of this and they're running out of that. Everything's turning to shit. Crazy folks in the street and poison in the air, Agent Orange and strontium 90. They'll kill you for your shoes up in this motherfucker! But we'll be okay under here. A man gets used to anything. The rats'll be along tonight, but they won't bother us. That clean dirt smell, you know? Just the same, if you got a steel jockstrap in your pack, better put it on! Just kidding, bro. The rats won't bother us. Unless you got crotch rot. You don't got it, do you? Crotch rot? If you do, better take a little sponge bath or something, because they'll be on you like trained dogs!"

.

5

WHAT ABOUT SOME BREAKFAST," Jack said the next morning. We went through a hole in the chain link fence and walked out to a little grove of squatty trees. A can opener, a safety razor and a jagged fragment of mirror glass dangled from strings tied to twigs, and a roll of toilet paper perched on a branch. A fire ring, water jugs, a few unopened cans of beans and a blackened coffee pot—it was a regular hobo jungle.

"Nice, Jack," I said. "All the comforts of home."

"Fuckin' A. If you want a shave, there's the mirror; you gotta take a shit, there's your toilet paper. If you want coffee we got that too. It's a fuckin' paradise, man."

Jack told me to sit tight for a bit. "I'm gonna get us some grub," he said. He walked away. I made a pot of coffee and started warming up a can of beans. Pretty soon Jack came back with two gallon wine jugs and not much else, or so it seemed. But then he unbuttoned his shirt, revealing steaks and pork chops plastered against his body.

"I hate to turn loose of this shit," he said, handing me a filet mignon. "Feels nice and cool on my skin, you know? Well, let's cook up."

Jack impaled several pork chops and steaks on a sharpened stick. We cracked open a jug of wine. After he got a few drinks under his belt, Jack was all for going back to Hollywood Boulevard.

"You wanna go over there by the yoga studio and scope out the cuties?"

"Fuck no. Why read the menu when you can't order the dinner?"

Besides, I had to think about making some money. I had a line on a gig as a sign spinner for a pizza dive. Not much of a job, but it was better than nothing. Or was it? The sun was beating down. The pork chops smelled great. I watched some ants scurrying up and down a tree trunk. So orderly, the ants, and so polite, always touching feelers every time they meet. "*Hi Joe! How's by you?*" Why can't people be more like that?

Then Angela happened along. "Trade you a blowjob for some food," she said. "Forget it," Jack said sharply. "You're just a kid. But you can eat with us if you want. We got plenty."

Angela really put it away. She must have been half starved. A john had dumped her in the desert, she said. She'd been walking for two days. She couldn't have been more than sixteen. I didn't ask for her back story. They're all the same, the life histories of the street girls. Almost before she's out of diapers she becomes a fucking block for the stepfather, the uncle or the father, and when she gets big enough she hits the road. It's a modern fairytale. The archetypal elements are all there: the dark forest, the humble cottage, the evil stepfather and the fair maiden, except that in today's version the maiden, instead of turning into a swan, dies in some nightmare alley with a needle in her arm.

We stuffed ourselves and then we stretched out in the weeds, patting our swollen bellies like aborigines. We were pretty looped, too. As I drifted off into a peaceful sleep I heard coyote howls, a distant train whistle and the dragonfly drone of a small plane sputtering high above our heads. You could hear birds singing too. It really was a paradise.

Days went by. Angela started living in the condemned building. Topside, I mean. We couldn't have her down below with us. Two homeless guys and an underage girl? Even though we weren't doing anything, if the cops busted us we'd be looking at some serious time. Jack found Angela a mattress, and someone gave her a beat-up chair. People were always giving her things. Everyone adored her. She knocked them out with her red plastic sparkle boots and her slinky faux fur boa. The old guy who owned the bodega down the block had a huge crush on her. He'd bring her a carne asada burrito and a rose from his garden just about every day. Some church ladies brought her a whole basket of egg salad sandwiches and a Bible. They meant well. Then she got a tiny dressing table with a cracked mirror at a yard sale. She had a pretty nice little setup. She'd bring her johns there in the daytime. She made money hand over fist. She wasn't stingy with it, either. She'd chip in big time with grocery money. We'd all go to Von's together. It was wonderfully cool in there with the air conditioning. We'd push our shopping cart just like regular folks, and Angela usually paid for everything. It even got to where Jack didn't have to shoplift anymore. All the same, he'd boost a filet mignon or a Delmonico steak now and then, just to keep his hand in.

Several nights around the campfire we were treated to spectacular sunsets, real cosmic nosebleeds. Red dribbled down from the sky and whooshing jets of yellow smog shot up from the great city reclining on its elbow in the distance. Whole sections of the horizon cracked open, spilling fiery incandescence on the trees. Everything turned salmon pink, the buildings fizzed orange and green, then suddenly the sky collapsed and it was over, just like that, and a dusty dull red baked-enamel haze settled over the world. The air grew still, and hundreds of tiny toads that lived in the black slag-oil puddles came hopping out—little fat bastards gorged with mosquito larvae—and they began their howling banshee chorus.

It was beautiful, except when Jack would get going about the revolution. That crap was wearing pretty thin with me, so one night I really lowered the boom on him.

"Let me ask you something, Jack. You were in the Army, right?"

"Yeah."

"What was your rank?"

"What do you mean?"

"Simple question. What was your rank?"

"Private. What about you?"

"Me too. Same thing. Private. So do you think when the revolution comes that they're going to make us second lieutenants? Is that what you think? You think they're going to hand us captain's bars? Do you think we're going to be riding in the club car and drinking champagne with the officers? We're dog soldiers, Jack. Cannon fodder. Do you really imagine that the cuties are going to go for guys like you and me? The *ragazze belle?* Dance every dance, will you, Jack? Breakfast at Tiffany's? Fly to Catalina for lunch? Life's not going to be any different for us, my friend. Life's not going to be any different, period. It'll be the same as it's always been, the haves and the have-nots, the serfs and the nobles, the masters and the slaves, the officers and the men, the sharecroppers and the plantation owners. It'll be the same old game of Chinese baseball: you play ball with them or they stick the bat up your ass."

We talked a lot about Tony, too, those nights around the campfire. Tony, that big tawny tiger. Tony, the Phantom of Lafayette Park. He'd slipped through our fingers, that much was sure. The quality woman in Brentwood? It was possible. Maybe she didn't dump him after all. Maybe the two of them were in Paris by now. Or maybe Tony was back in the Big Apple, the cellar bar on Houston, tickling the keys with his fast hands, with his big padded tiger paws. I wanted to ask Jack straight out, "Did Tony really fight Jake LaMotta in the Garden?" but I already knew the answer, because I'd done the research at the wifi on Fairfax, and I'd done the math, too. But I didn't want to burst Jack's bubble. Besides, I was feeling bad because I'd unloaded on him earlier about the revolution. Jack lived in a dream world; he was the Francois Villon of his own imagination. Pathological lying was a lot more than a hobby with Jack. It was more than a sport, more than recreational therapy, even. It was his vocation. Jack was like a spider spinning a delicate web of fantasy. That fine spun dream world was Jack's buffer zone, his cocoon. It was all he had between himself and the tarantula reality of the street.

Jack and I got to wondering also why the cops didn't roust Angela out every night along with the other squatters. We asked her about it one day on the way back from Von's.

"I suck their dicks," she explained.

I GOT MY BIG INNING with a quality woman in Brentwood, just like Tony, but in typical fashion, I fucked it up. It happened like this. I sold my wedding ring for 30 bucks, and then I went to Cole's, where Jimmy D and I used to hang out. That's where I met Papageorgopoulou.

"Call me George," he said. We were having a beer at the bar. I was watching my money because I wanted to be able to order a decent meal and not worry when it came to paying the bill. I wanted to feel like a human being, if only for an hour or so. At the same time I could have kicked myself because I should have known when I watched that scrunched-up little monkey behind the counter squinting at my goods through his loupe that he'd rip me off. Wedding rings don't bring much these days on South Broadway.

Papageorgopoulou, George, was a gigolo, the real thing. He told me how he'd trawl the Internet personals for rich skirts. He was handsome as hell, and there was something about his quirky mustache and the way he flashed his teeth at you. He had that 'bad boy' look. The cuties were nuts about him.

"Say, what does a guy like you do for poon?" he asked me.

"Poon?"

"Quiff, quail, bush, ginch, coochie."

"You mean girls?"

We ordered lunch. Papageorgopoulou got the Swiss steak and I got the beef stuffed cabbage with mashed potatoes and coleslaw. Papageorgopoulou paid. He said he had a prospect for me. He wanted to hand me down one of his Brentwood ladies.

"She's not exactly young," he cautioned over dessert. "I want you to understand that from the start."

"George, I don't know…"

"Bullshit," he said. He ordered two more beers. "It's all about confidence. I'm handing you a goldmine, man. I like you. I want to see you turn your life around. I wouldn't be telling you this if I didn't think you could do it. Put on your game face, bro. You'll be on the green in three."

I went to the can. I was feeling pretty nervous, but I knew I had to give it a go. Any port in a storm! I took a peek at myself in the mirror. Confidence? My pants were held up with safety pins. And where did I get that hat? Can't remember. What a disaster. Give the world half a chance and it'll wipe the floor with your ass.

I went back to the bar. Papageorgopoulou was writing down the doll's address and phone number on a piece of paper.

"Come on," he said. "What have you got to lose?"

He had me there.

We took a taxi to his pad and he kicked down some duds for me, designer labels. He was one of the nicest guys I ever met, Papageorgopoulou. Of course I was doing him a favor, in a way, taking that Brentwood cutie off his hands.

We said goodbye and I caught the #21 up to Rampart

with my new finery in a shopping bag. My plan was to drop in on my old pal Bobbo so I could take a shower and get changed and spruced up for my meeting with the quality woman.

Bobbo was a strange one. He was a day sleeper, always 'going down for his nap.' He claimed it was narcolepsy. His day was one long siesta. He'd lie doggo for weeks until his SSI check came in. Only one thing could rouse Bobbo from his lethargy: speed, crank, methedrine. I'd drive him to Uncle Barney's in the van. This was the same Uncle Barney who was Kenji's connect. Bobbo lived with his moms. They were very poor and regularly ate canned dog food. After Uncle Barney's I'd stay at Bobbo's for a meal, a shower and a sleepover. For dinner we'd have Alpo Chunky Beef over noodles, or more often the Alpo Ground Puppy Formula with Chicken and Rice. It turned my stomach, but beggars can't be choosers. Moms sometimes made what she called her homemade stockpot soup. It was actually a mixture of several kinds of the Campbell's junk thrown together in a big pot. I know because I'd look through the trash and find the empty cans. The worst thing we had was Chef Boyardee Spaghetti, thick soft noodles like decayed worms and tiny meatballs the size of rabbit turds. Even the Alpo was better than that.

After dinner we'd sit in the living room and Moms would get in on the conversation. She still had hopes for Bobbo.

"I keep telling him to go up to Alaska and get on one of those fishing boats. It's hard work, but boy, do they make the money!"

"Those ads are fake, Mom. It's lists. All they're selling is lists. It's a scam. Don't you know that? It's a fucking scam."

"It's not a scam and watch your language, Honey. It's in the newspaper. They can't put fake ads in the newspaper. It's against the law." Then, as an aside, to me:

"He never used to use that language. I don't know where he picked those words up. Certainly not from you. You're a real gentleman! I appreciate the way you've taken an interest in him. You're a good influence. He always perks up when you're around. I always thought that maybe he'd be a writer. Or a philosopher. He wrote a lovely essay about Alfred North Whitehead when he was a junior in high school. It won a prize. In fact, Jerzy, I'd like you to read it. I'd like to get your opinion. I think we still have it here somewhere."

"Mom, that was thirty years ago."

And she'd go on like this, on and on, talking about him in the third person, just like he wasn't there, which, in a very real sense, he wasn't.

Moms took exception to Bobbo's peeing outdoors. "He pees outdoors at night when he's watching television," she told me. "Don't say you don't, Honey. I can hear you in my bedroom, right through the window. Why do men do that? Why is it so important to men to pee outdoors? My father used to pee outdoors, in the fields, but we lived on a farm…"

I tried my damnedest to explain it to her.

"Peeing outdoors? It has to do with the groundwater. I mean, you think of your urine seeping down, filtered through sand and gravel, right down to the bedrock. It's returning one's essence to the elements, a sort of mystical participation, I guess. You piss on the earth, a chorus of frog cheeps goes up, you're helping things along. You're putting in your two cents, so to speak. It's mysterious. The associations, I mean. Just words, sometimes, the way they sound. A word like aquifer," for instance. Or silica. Or the concept of an artesian well. I don't know how to explain it. We're talking about an organic connection with the earth. You know Wordsworth's lines, '…rolled around in earth's diurnal course, with rocks, and stones, and trees?' It's like that."

When Moms would leave the room Bobbo would fix,

then, alert and bushy-tailed as a hotwired squirrel, he'd start in. With his plans, I mean, for the future.

"Welding school! That's the real deal. You know it? Twenty-four months and you get your certificate. I wish to Christ I'd done that when I was young, but what the fuck? It's never too late. You can turn your life around at any age. You know what I'm saying?"

"Yeah, sure."

"Do you remember in *Lawrence of Arabia,* where General Allenby says to Lawrence, 'You're the most extraordinary man I ever met?' I felt at that moment like he was talking directly to me. I really did. I've got my faults, sure, we all do, but I'm a human being! I'm a human being, with dreams and aspirations. I'm an extraordinary man. I really am. By Christ, I know it in my heart."

"Yeah, well…"

"And welding, yes sir, welding is something you can get your hands into, you know? It's real work. This white-collar shit is work, but it's not *work* work. You know what I mean? You've worked in these fucking offices. You've seen the goddamn shit that goes down. It's bullshit, man! Bunch of nancy boys, afraid to get their hands dirty. You hang around the water cooler and talk about who's sucking who off. The truth of it is that they're all sucking each other off 24-7, the lousy cocksuckers. I'm through with that shit, man. Been there, done that and adios motherfuckers! A man's gotta work with his hands."

Next on the agenda was usually the dog, Denise. The Little Pisser, he called her. She was a dirty little thing about the size of a Norwegian rat, and the stink of her was rank.

"It's her mouth. Her teeth are rotting away. See how loose they are? *The Little Pisser!*" He pulls back the dog's lips, causing her to grimace horribly, like a miniature hyena. "See that yellow coating on her tongue? You see it? The sticky stuff? Bacteria, whole colonies. She's infested. Look at her. You see what she's doing? She's laughing at us! She loves creeping us out, the little fucking bitch. She's perverse, twisted. But it's not her fault."

It was truly heartbreaking when he'd talk about the Little Pisser's puppy days.

"When we first got her from those shit-lovers at the trailer park she was almost catatonic. She was just a puppy, man! They batted her around like a ping-pong ball, the white trash motherfuckers. Christ, what a world!"

Sometimes at this point the dog, perched on his lap, would make a strange noise, halfway between a bark and a burp.

"She's dyspeptic, too. Is that the word? She belches and belches. Her guts are rotten. Cancer. She's riddled with it. Ruptured uterus, ovarian cysts, pinworms, you name it, brother. Did you ever smell her burps? Jesus, God! Makes you want to puke! Her farts are even worse. Boy, if you want to smell something wicked! Fuckin' stink bombs from hell, dawg. But you should see her when she shits. The pinworms, I'm talking about. Her goddamn shit's alive with the little fuckers. Twisting, squirming, crawling all over each other like fuckin' live spaghetti! Say, did you know that human beings have pinworms too? Sure! Everybody's got them; you, me, the guy down the block, even your goddamn cuties from Agoura Hills and Thousand Oaks. Pinworms! They crawl out of your asshole at night while you're asleep and lay their eggs on your fucking pillowcase."

It was funny about Denise, the Little Pisser. We came back from Uncle Barney's one night and Bobbo strangled her. He cried about it later. He claimed he loved the Little Pisser, and I believed him. He was tweaked, that's the only excuse I can think of. It was the speed. "If only she hadn't farted at that particular instant," he muttered. Moms took it pretty hard, and I felt sorry for her. We told Moms that Denise had simply dropped dead, probably a heart attack, and she bought it. We buried the little body in the back yard.

Uncle Barney lived with his moms too. She was ninety-eight and he was sixty-seven. Their pad was claustrophobic. Narrow corridors between five-foot stacks of bundled newspapers and National Geographics led to the kitchen and bathroom. Rabbit runs is what they were, those corridors. And the stacks were alive with silverfish and brown recluse spiders.

"You should see the love dance of the silverfish," Uncle Barney told us. "It's really poignant. First, the male and female stand face to face, with their antennae touching. Then the male beats a retreat and the female chases him. In the third phase, the two of them stand side by side, in the 69 position, with the male vibrating his tail. He's giving her the business, you see."

Uncle Barney had collapsed veins, as well as a variety of other ailments. He couldn't slam the stuff anymore so they'd chase the dragon, the two of them, Uncle Barney and Bobbo, while I sat at the kitchen table with Moms drinking hot Ovaltine and leafing through the National Geographics.

Uncle Barney lived almost entirely in the past.

"Ah, the changes I've seen! When I was young the Kennedy Administration answered to the Gambino Family and that was it. Simple. Today what's left of the Gambino Family answers to the Texas oil families and the Texas oil families answer to the Elders of Zion and the Elders of Zion answer to the Saudi princes and we're all just threads in Osama's prayer rug. We're nothing but hairs in Bin Laden's beard! I'll tell you one thing: In the twenty-first century, the world will dance to the Binster's tune or it won't dance at all. He's the Hurdy-Gurdy Man, no mistake about it. We'll do the monkey dance while he twangs the strings of his famous Kalashnikov, eight to the bar, dawg! *Eight to the bar!* Rat-tat-tat! But I look back to the old days. I mean, you knew where you stood with Carlo Gambino. He was ruthless, but he was fair. You know what I'm saying? Those were the days, my friends."

One day, or one night, rather, a homeless man was

pinched for jerking off in front of the Victoria's Secret window, corner of Hollywood and Highland. The incident made the papers.

"You can well understand how it might have happened," Uncle Barney said. "I mean, those lifelike mannequins with their sassy expressions and their faux diamond teddies! Holy fucking Christ! You've seen them! It could happen to anybody, you know? Say you were standing there at two in the morning in front of the Victoria's Secret window, homeless and drunk and half crazy with loneliness and despair, and without your hardly being aware of it your hand strays down to your fly, and before you know it you're jerking yourself silly and you splooge all over the window. *That window!* The Victoria's Secret window! It's the emblem of the world, man, that window. *You can look but you can't touch.* Take me, for example. I mean, shit, let's face it, I'm sixty-seven years old! The only way I'm ever going to get laid again is to pay a lot of money or commit some dreadful crime."

6

ANYWAY, a meal, a shower and a sleepover. We had the fucking Chef Boyardee Spaghetti for dinner that night but it was wonderful sleeping in a bed, and the next morning I got duded up in my Armani and Tommy Hilfiger rags and borrowed a pair of wingtips from Bobbo. Those shoes were in great shape because he rarely left the house. I still had most of the thirty bucks I'd gotten for the ring, so I bought a pint of whiskey and got on a bus for Brentwood. I had cold feet, but I knew I had to go through with it. *"Confidence! It's all about confidence,"* I told myself between sips of Ancient Age.

My quality woman, Corliss...that was her name, Corliss. Papageorgopoulou was right. She wasn't young. Her hands were fish-belly white and they were speckled with brown spots. She had peach fuzz on her cheeks and an eye that wandered. Nevertheless, it all went swimmingly at first. She moved me into the pool shed and set me up with a computer and all. She started me out writing her autobiography. She'd record her shticks and I'd transcribe it from a disk. It was great fun being on the Internet, although I freely admit that I spent too much time at porn sites like *Barely Legal Cheerleaders*.

I did all the cooking. Her favorite dish was braised

radicchio with raisins and pine nuts. She bought me a green silk Hokusai print kimono, an Italian sauté pan and a Masamoto sushi knife.

The sun even shines on a dog's ass once in a while.

At night you could see the moon and the stars. I'd sit under the grape arbor with a bottle of Château Haut-Beauséjour white Bordeaux, looking out over Pacific Palisades and Topanga Canyon, and I'd be thinking, here I am in Brentwood, a weevil in the flour, a rat in the cheese, and it's glorious. Beautiful Shiny People of Brentwood, I've managed to tunnel under your wallpaper! Toddle downstairs for a midnight snack, switch on the light, and you'll see me, fat and sassy, running up your kitchen wall. You'd squash me if you could, wouldn't you? Of course you would. *Come on, admit it!* Because I don't live anywhere in particular, I live everywhere. You'll find me in your soup, on your toothbrush, under your fingernails. I'm the lint in your navel, the fungus between your toes. I'm *Demodex Folliculorum*, the mite that eats your eyebrows, I'm that forty-foot tapeworm coiled up in your intestines, laughing like an evil genie.

There was one girl at the *Barely Legal Cheerleaders* site who had the cutest little pink and white pompoms, bunny puffs, on her sneakers. I just couldn't get enough of her. I thought of Uncle Barney's derelict splooging on the Victoria's Secret window. *You can look but you can't touch!* And here I am up in Brentwood splooging all over my 42-inch plasma screen. It took complete possession of me, the masturbatory madness. I turned myself inside out, like a starfish. I thought I'd never stop squirting. My God, what a rush! I jerked myself silly. It was one of the happiest weeks of my life. Corliss would come out and look in on me, bring me a new disk, and her quivering nostrils would pick up the raw protein odor of fresh-pumped sperm. I thought she was going to tackle me right then and there.

Then she started lurking around the grape arbor at night in a pink chemise. I didn't know if I was supposed to shtup her off or what. To shtup or not to shtup? It's hard to get a handle on these things sometimes. I suppose you'll think I'm naïve, but I'd never been anybody's boy-toy before. Then too, I'm not like those handsome guys, the real gigolos in their silk kimonos, always ready to rip off a little biz between the braised radicchio and the filet mignon au poivre. I mean, my pecker isn't something that's perpetually charged up and ready to go, like a cattle prod. *Sorry, Papageorgopoulou, old pal!* I'm afraid I wasn't much of a gigolo. To be perfectly honest, it wasn't so much the peach fuzz on her cheeks or the funny eye as those brown trout hands of hers. Those Dolly Varden hands! I just didn't fancy her touching me with them. Besides, I wasn't at all sure she wasn't a man. In LA you never know what you're going to find inside a pair of designer panties.

To make a long story short, I didn't get the money and I didn't get the power and I didn't get the woman. Jack and Angela were glad to see me back at the old homestead, and the truth is I was glad to see them, too.

IT STARTED OUT with wanting to take a bath, the three of us. It had been weeks for me, and months, or maybe even years for Jack, and for Angela who knows? I had my own signature stench. They say a woodchuck always smells his own hole first, but the truth is you're not aware of your own stink. You're immersed in it, just like a fish is immersed in water. Jack, for example, had a signature stench. By that I mean an aroma that pertained to Jack and to nobody else. You walk down the street and you smell a certain smell and you say, "Somebody's frying bacon!" Or you smell something else and you say, "That's horse shit!" Same thing with Jack. Your nostrils pick up a fierce eye-watering stench, and you say, "That's Jack!"

Anyway, Jack had a pal, Brad, who worked as a busboy at the North Hollywood Holiday Inn on Vineland, and he'd hook us up so we could take a dip in the Jacuzzi. It sounded fine, but we needed better clothes if we were going to pass for tourists at the Holiday Inn. It had been ages since my sojourn in Brentwood and my trendy Armani and Tommy Hilfiger duds had pretty much rotted off me. When you're homeless you don't really change your clothes the way regular people do. You simply molt, like a rattlesnake or a Gila monster. Anyway, I was a mess. My Third Army field jacket was black with dirt and I'd gone back to wearing the pants with the safety pins. *And Jack!* Jack's shirt was ragged and his pants were torn. I mean, you could see his wedding tackle. Angela, of course, looked fine. Her johns were always buying her cute little outfits. We all went to the Deseret Industries Thrift Store and got Jack and me some new clothes, with Angela shelling out.

The next day was Sunday. We took a bus to North Hollywood. Before we left we made Angela promise that she wouldn't go turning tricks at the Holiday Inn and blow our cover. I caught a glimpse of our reflections in a fancy dress shop window as we walked along Vineland and sure enough, we really did look like ordinary citizens.

Everything went off like clockwork. Brad let us into the Jacuzzi area and brought us some lovely little cakes of soap. We had bathing suits underneath our clothes. The hot water felt great and we scrubbed and scrubbed. I felt layers of dirt coming off as well as layers of desolation and despair. It's amazing what living like a human being for an hour will do for your morale. When Jack got into the Jacuzzi the water turned black. I'm not exaggerating. It was like his pores were secreting octopus ink. I got a surprise, too. I'd always made Jack out to be Syrian or Lebanese, but he turned out to be just your ordinary garden-variety white man.

What an angel Brad was! After our bath he brought us some thick white towels. Then we got dressed in the lobby bathrooms. Now it was time for the continental breakfast. We stuffed ourselves with scrambled eggs and croissants.

Then I conked off in a comfy chair with the kissy, dovey musak in my ears, a peaceful dreamless sleep.

When I woke up the women's restroom door across the lobby had just opened and out stepped a stunning Chinese girl in sheer turquoise harem pants and a cobwebby white sweater. Absolutely scrumptious, just the sort of caviar a fellow wants to put on his cracker. She smiled invitingly, her sparkling black eyes met mine—and for a brief hallucinating instant I thought she was going reach out and take my hand.

Have you been waiting long, Darling? No Babycakes, not long. *Dearest, you're wearing a new cologne.* Aramis For Men, Honey Bunny. *Care for a mint, Snookums?* Thank you, Pumpkin. *Do you mind driving, Lambchop?* No, of course not, my Little Tiramisu...

I conked off again and again I woke up. This time it was Jack, tapping on my shoulder. "Angela's MIA," he said. "She'll blow our cover!" Just then Angela stepped out of the elevator, looking flushed and rumpled.

"I told you," Jack said. "She got herself a john."

I was frosted. "Jesus Christ, Angela," I said. "You promised—"

"Chill the fuck out," Angela said. "I gave him a blowjob in the men's toilet." She flashed two crisp Benjamins. "Come on, I'm taking us to the movies. *The Road to Perdition* is playing at the New World Cinema." Angela was in a buoyant mood.

"New World Cinema," Jack said. "That's all the way over in Venice Beach!"

"Fuck it," Angela chirped. "We'll take a taxi..."

We pulled off this Holiday Inn caper several more times until Brad was pinched on a parole violation. It turned out that Brad had done three years at Chino for armed robbery. He looked like a fresh-faced college kid, but as the saying goes, you can't always judge by appearances.

MORNING. PERSHING SQUARE. The Violin Lady, that squatty little gargoyle, her birdseed eyes darting like pinwheels, mutters obscenities into her beard as she feeds her pigeons. An old man sitting on a bench, staring at his hands, waiting for a miracle—or for the second coming of Christ. A few sleeping derelicts, covered with filthy rags and damp newspapers, as if the sewer had erupted during the night and vomited its leavings—these shipwrecked human beings—on the grass. Just across the street, the luxurious Biltmore Hotel, which looks out on Pershing Square. Inside, no doubt, the soft tinkle of silverware, the murmur of subdued conversation, waiters hurrying with rashers of bacon and pouring steaming hot coffee from silver pitchers. Los Angeles is becoming more and more like Calcutta every day. It's true when you think about it. Because in India, if you get bored sitting around your hotel room, you can always go out and watch somebody die in the street.

At Pershing Square I met Félix—"Felo"—Santiago from the Dominican. He ran a demolition crew. He said he might need workers and he gave me his card. A few days went by and I figured I'd better call Felo while my clothes still looked halfway decent. I gave him a jingle and he told me to report to a site on Wilshire near Korea Town. It happened that Jack's dance card wasn't filled up, so I brought him along with me and we both got hired.

It was a sweet deal. We'd go to a site where the wrecking ball had been swinging for days. Sometimes the crane operator was still there, inside his little square tractor. The ball would swing, and it was thrilling to see the walls collapse, the bricks fall and the tall plumes of dust rise into the air.

Once the wrecking ball had done its work, we'd wade in with our tools. Felo, his brother, Jack, myself and another flunky, a Colombian called Piojo. Sledgehammers, crowbars, wrecking bars. We'd knock down the walls, smash the windows, and pry up the floorboards. My appetite for destruction was boundless. I looked forward to going to work each day. I would have done it for nothing.

At night I dreamed that I was a giant in seven league boots, swinging an enormous wrecking bar and a stupendous transcontinental hammer. I demolished the entire civilized world, reduced it to rubble: the Eiffel Tower, Yankee Stadium, the Parthenon, the Kremlin, the Washington Monument, London Bridge.

I thought I'd found my calling for sure, but there was a downside to it. Every so often a shiny new car would pull up. It was the Beautiful People, the Starbuck's set. Piojo would go trotting out, and money changed hands. Obviously, Felo was dealing, and judging by the pretty shiny people who were his customers, it figured to be yayo. Then five guys from Compton started stopping by in a pink Cadillac. They were strapped and one of them had a scorpion tattoo in the middle of his forehead. Jack and I were feeling pretty antsy. I tried to talk to Piojo about it, but it was impossible. Piojo was a deaf mute; he wrote everything down on a little slate that hung from his neck on a dirty cord. When I told him we were scared, he wrote 'Fuck You' on the slate in big letters.

In order to be near the job, Jack and I got a room on Rampart. After work we'd sometimes catch the Wilshire bus and go to the New Beverly Cinema near Hancock Park, where they show the old movies. We watched *Key Largo* and *Little Caesar*. We were both crazy about Edward G. Robinson, yesterday's Carlito Brigante. I thought about Dionisio. Nabbed and deported? Gunned down by the cops? Or was he raking it in at *El Paraisio*? We saw *Casablanca* and *The Big Sleep*, too. Tony had pretty much dropped off the radar, but we'd go by Lafayette Park nearly every day to look for him.

Jack and I were becoming upwardly mobile, but our new digs were less than ideal. The neighborhood was claustrophobic, and there was so much graffiti you felt like you were living inside a can of alphabet soup. We were right in the middle of Little Central America. You could hear automatic weapons fire at night. Our roommate was an Egyptian. No English. There were three of us crammed into a tiny single room. Plus the Egyptian was a somnambulist, a sleepwalker. He barged around the room at all hours of the night, knocking everything over, and muttering, muttering. We couldn't tell what he was saying, but it sounded like an incantation. He had a bowl of some kind of stuff that he stirred with a big screwdriver. We called him Mr. Mumbles, the Egyptian Mummy Man.

Then, after only a month had gone by, our boss Felo was killed in a driveby and the job abruptly ended. We still had a little money but we didn't know what to do. Then those five torpedoes from Compton showed up in their pink Cadillac. We figured Piojo must have dimed us out. We didn't have anything to hide, but just the same, we were plenty spooked.

"You know," Jack said, "I think we were better off in Boyle Heights."

I agreed. It was time to cut a chogie. We climbed out an upstairs window, skipped out on the rent. It was a rotten trick to play on Mr. Mumbles, but we were desperate.

It turned out that we got back to Boyle Heights just in time to say our goodbyes to Angela. She'd been adopted by an old pedophile, a retired cinematographer. For Angela, it was the opportunity of a lifetime. She'd have it all: a beautiful home in Agoura Hills, a pool, a Jacuzzi, and they'd shop together for her clothes on Rodeo Drive. Of course she'd have to give up her rights as a human being. She'd be a sex slave. But I knew I didn't have to worry about Angela. Angela was a survivor. She'd taken to the streets when she was twelve years old because it was better than being gang-raped every day by her uncle, her stepfather and the three stepbrothers. This girl knew how to soldier. If they gave out medals for living in the street,

Angela would have gotten the Silver Star.

Jack and I went to Von's and picked up some Korbel's brut. We bought it; we didn't boost it. No more shoplifting for us. That was part of our new affluent lifestyle. We sat in creaky chairs around Angela's dressing table with the cracked mirror. An old scarecrow called the Pied Piper was slumped in a corner tugging on a bottle of Mad Dog 20/20, so we invited him to join us. We called him the Pied Piper because he was a rat catcher. He had traps set out all over the building. You had to be careful where you stepped, especially if you weren't wearing shoes. He'd roast the rats outside, on a spit. He'd caught and cooked up several dogs, too, little ones, strays. He told us he got started eating dog in Nam. Claimed it wasn't bad once you got past that "doggy" taste.

Before we'd finished the champagne the chicken hawk from Agoura Hills pulled up in his Black Sapphire BMW. He looked like any old geezer, double chin, puffy eyes. We went outside. I felt like I was sending a daughter off to finishing school.

Angela gave me a big hug and she puddled up, too.

"You got a lotta sparkle, Kid," I said.

Angela hugged Jack and started toward the car. "You two are the best friends I ever had," she murmured. "I'll never forget you."

7

I GOT OUT OF THERE TOO, at least for a while. Okay, it's decided, I said, I'm going to San Francisco. I still had a few bucks left from the demolition job. I gathered up my bedroll and packed a canvas gym bag with a few things.

It's amazing, I told myself, what a change of scene will do for your morale. And I badly needed a change. I was becoming invisible. On my solitary walks through the city, from Arco Plaza to Lafayette Park, up and down Hollywood Boulevard, I found myself forever peering in shop windows, not in the windows, exactly, but at the surface of the glass, to see if my image was reflected there. Did I exist at all? Or had I completely disintegrated?

Union Station, with its cavernous waiting room and gleaming tiled floors, is such a glorious place that I was almost sorry when it came time to board my train. I was feeling better already. Los Angeles' Union Station is a magnificent anachronism, a temple built by a vanished race of giants and dedicated to an unknown god, a reminder that there once was a time when human beings mattered and life had purpose and meaning.

Aboard the Amtrak now. Gliding along. A gin and tonic. Silently gliding. Reminds me of the Eurorail. *Gleis.*

That's the word you hear in all the banhoffs. *Gleis*. Perfect word, *gleis*. Perfectly describes the sensation. Gliding along, not a care in the world. Still healthy, still optimistic. Trees and buildings flying by outside the window. At least there are still a few trees left in the world. Not a bad world when you have money in your pocket. Beautiful world, actually. *Gleis, gleis*. My past life is being erased. Another gin and tonic. The fraulein across the aisle just crossed her legs. Smiled at me, too. Or maybe I imagined it. But what does it matter? Does anything matter? Eighty thousand people crushed to death in an earthquake the other day. Pakistan, I think it was. If eighty thousand people can be swept away like a hatch of grasshoppers, what do the problems of one little person matter? The gin is booming in my veins. God, I feel good. She smiled at me again. I'm sure of it now. Birth, copulation, death. You come out of one hole and you end up in another one. It's a pretty short trip. You get on the train and you get off. How far, I wonder, metaphorically speaking? Bremerhaven to Dusseldorf, let's say. Shorter than that even. Mannheim to Stuttgart. A pretty short trip. You get on the train and you get off. What's the meaning of it all? Why should life have a meaning? What's the meaning of a peach? Why worry about it? Bremerhaven to Dusseldorf. Why worry about anything? Still healthy, still optimistic. Wildly optimistic, I would even say. Shit, I haven't felt this optimistic in years. Gliding along. Leaving it all behind, the idiot entanglements, the problems, the worries. I feel absolutely marvelous.

It's been my experience in life that if you step back and simply allow events to take their course, things will usually work out okay.

Or they won't.

8

SAN FRANCISCO—Fisherman's Wharf, Russian Hill, the cable cars—it's a beautiful town if you have money, and I didn't so I ended up back at Boyle Heights. Some weeks passed and Jack disappeared for a while and the food supply dried up. One morning I was walking along Broadway, famished. I hardly knew where I was. Suddenly a squarely built man in cook's whites stepped out of a doorway and seized my shoulder in a powerful grip.

"You help me move steam tebble," he said. "You come. I show."

Like a predator, this meatball dragged me inside a cafe, Mike's Diner, and before I knew it I was lifting a steam table, a chopping block, a giant mixer, a broiler and an oven, several steel cabinets, huge kettles, and dozens of sacks of potatoes and flour. We hustled this stuff from one side of the cafe, which was apparently being remodeled, to the other. Intermittently, as we lurched and grunted and struggled, Mike (so his nametag read) continued to cook breakfast for his patrons, seated at a counter, assisted by a fetching young waitress in a short tight skirt.

During a pause in the proceedings, Mike suddenly handed me a heavy kettle that he lifted easily. The kettle immediately slipped through my fingers and clattered on the floor, almost smashing my toes. I couldn't grip the kettle as Mike did. His hands were enormous, his fingers like bratwursts. He was about sixty, with a head like a bullet. I noticed that he wore a hearing aid. He looked like a big evil monkey with shiny steel-rimmed glasses and a starched cook's hat.

Finally it was over. I plopped down at the counter, next to one of the customers, who was busy shoveling it in. "I've just made myself five bucks," I'm thinking proudly. But no. Mike nods brusquely at me, wiping off his spatula with a dirty towel. "You can go now."

"Bull*shit!*" I say, rising to my feet. "I helped you out. You pay me something, bro. I'm hungry."

Mike gazed at me evenly, his steely eyes glinting behind the shiny glasses. I thought for a moment that he was going to hit me, but suddenly, without a word, he turned on his heel and stepped to the grill. Moments later he returned with three eggs over easy, hash browns, bacon, toast and coffee. He slammed the plates down in front of me, then he stood there, arms folded, like a foreman, ready to make sure I ate it all.

I didn't disappoint him. In seconds, I put the breakfast away. He came back at me with a plate of meatloaf, mashed potatoes, gravy, a roll, and diced carrots and peas. This too, I gulped down in record time. Next, he slammed down a bowl of cabbage soup. Not bad, homemade, it was the real thing. At last I was getting full.

"What's for dessert?" I asked confidently, shoving the empty soup bowl away.

"What you want?" Mike said, glaring at me like an inquisitor.

"Apple pie and ice cream."

"No ice cream."

Mike gave me a tiny sliver of apple pie, which I swallowed in a single bite. Delicious. With a meal under my belt, I was feeling great.

"You beeg man. You eat good, yes?"

"Yes. How about some more coffee?"

Mike poured, sloshing some hot coffee on my hand—purposely, it seemed to me. I saw the move coming and didn't flinch. Mike looked at me keenly. His expression was malicious, monkeylike, mean, tricky, sly. I finished my coffee and wiped my mouth and got up to leave.

"I need man in kitchen," Mike said. "Strong man. Heavy work. I pay good. You eat here. Best food in town. Mike's Diner. My name is Mike. What you say?"

I said yes and held out my hand. That was a mistake. Mike crushed my fingers in a powerful grip. The man was brutally strong. Several seconds went by and he refused to let go. He was enjoying my discomfort. The pain was excruciating. I thought about grabbing a fork and jabbing it into his eye. A sly smile crept across the brute's face and he glanced at the waitress as if to say, 'I'm still king of the mountain here.'

So began my stint at Mike's Diner. I helped finish up the remodeling, peeled potatoes, mixed pancake batter, cleaned the grease trap, scrubbed the grill, washed the pots and pans, mopped the floor and carried out the garbage. The walls of the kitchen were plastered with pages torn from girlie magazines, beaver shots. "I like women," Mike said to me. There was a permanent sign in the window: "Waitress Wanted." In addition to Graciela, the waitress I met on the first day, there was a steady stream of young girls. Two days seemed to be the usual turnaround time. I guess that's how long it took Mike to make his move.

Always, the routine was the same. He put them into the standard uniform: a see-through seersucker blouse and a short tight skirt. A day passed, he tried something, she got mad, he roughed her up, and then she left. Mike was like a rhinoceros in heat. Diplomacy and congeniality were not a part of his makeup.

Mike always left the door of the can open when he took a piss, as a sort of invitation to the dolls. It sounded like he was shooting a fire hose into the toilet bowl. He must have been hung like a horse. No wonder the girls were afraid of him. Everyone was. The customers ate with their heads bowed, completely subdued, meek as field mice, their eyes glued to their plates.

Mike was a dynamite keg ready to go off at any moment. He loved to startle people. He'd slap a heavy dinner plate down on the counter next to a patron's elbow, then, while a malicious grin slowly spread across his mean monkey-like face, he'd fix the individual with a steady, mocking gaze, as if to say: 'Want to do something about it?'

He was full of sly tricks, always attempting to provoke me in subtle ways. Once, as he chopped a head of cabbage in half with a razor-sharp cleaver, inches away from my fingers, he said: "You see that? Thess how I chop anybody who try to take you away from these place."

Another time I tried to pass by him in the pantry. It was close quarters, and he didn't turn aside. I ran into his shoulder. It was like slamming into a steel girder. *Iron Mike!* We were the same height, yet he outweighed me by a good fifty or sixty pounds, and there wasn't an ounce of fat on him. Many times, when I watched him tying his apron around his narrow waist, I thought: *What a gorilla!* The difference in our physiques was due to his bone structure. Mike—Iron Mike—was built like a draft horse. He was a Michelangelo figure. His bones were girders, I-beams, two-by-fours. The muscles and sinews that clung to those bones were steel cables. His triceps were thick, twisted hawsers. Iron Mike was a very scary dude. Whenever he got especially cantankerous, he would turn his hearing aid down and shout at us in Polish.

Then there was the radio. The radio was tuned to a Slavic music station. It was the polka stuff plus a lot of sententious pitter-patter. Because of Mike's hearing problem, he kept the volume turned up loud. The fucking radio drove us nuts, but of course nobody dared touch it. It would have meant our jobs or worse.

Fortunately, I was able to take frequent breaks. I'd step outside and watch the women stitching at their sewing machines in the windows of sweatshops across the street. The diner was perched on the edge of the garment district, next door to the Las Palmas dancehall. Directly adjacent to the sweatshops across the street was the old United Artists Building with its frieze of soulful dryads and nereids and its ornate rusty crown.

Sometimes I hid out in the pantry, hoping to make time with Graciela or one of the new girls. Often, when I was alone in the pantry, trying to decide what to do with my life, I heard a rustling and a scampering among the bags of potatoes and pancake flour. The place was alive with rats and mice.

Graciela was crazy about onions. Whenever she chopped the vegetables she was constantly pinching up a bit of raw onion and stuffing it into her mouth. More than once I saw her pick up a peeled onion and bite into it as if it were an apple.

One day I was staggering past the sink with a one hundred pound bag of potatoes on my shoulder when Graciela suddenly threw her arms around me and kissed me. Her mouth tasted like onions. Her apron was saturated with blood. She'd been standing at the butcher's bench smacking out hamburger patties.

She pulls up her apron and skirt and presses her twat against my knuckles. All afire, I dump my bag of potatoes on the floor. I bend her back over the sink and kiss her again and again. Her hair is dipping in the dishwater. She's tugging at my pants. I'm breathing like a racehorse. Suddenly we hear Mike lumbering and grumbling. *The motherfucker!* He smells a rat. Graciela grabs my cock and jerks it, and I squirt all over her beautiful big legs and her bloody apron.

Next day, a new girl. Hortensia or Ofelia. No English. But what tits! She was constantly cracking her gum. It sounded like her teeth were exploding. She French kissed me in the pantry. The sugary smell of her breath was intoxicating. I lifted her up—she was just a little thing— and plunked her down on the chopping block. In an instant I had her tits out. I wanted to get my mouth on her boobs but I couldn't stop kissing her. As I squeezed her nipples she pursed her lips and shot her wad of gum into my mouth. It was Juicy Fruit.

"*Papacito*," she murmured hoarsely, moving her lips against my teeth, "*Papacito*..."

She fumbled with my shirt buttons, her eyes orgasmic. Suddenly—the lumbering and grumbling. Mike again. This time it was a close call, very close. I knew I was pushing the envelope and I began to wonder how long I could keep it up. The last thing in the world I wanted was to tangle ass with that gorilla.

The following day—I couldn't wait to get to work— Graciela was back. Entranced, I watched her standing at the butcher's bench, grinding the hamburger. She moved her hips in rhythm with the cranking action of the grinder while her hands caressed the glistening column of red meat that was spurting out of the steel chute. I sensed the inevitability of our union, as if I were reading a railroad timetable. In my mind I could see her coming at me, sliding down the rails. We're going to be hooking up, pronto, just like two cars in the yard. I can feel us snapping together, tongue and groove. She's lubricated with railroad grease, and I'm socking it to her. Holy Jesus! This is the bonus hamburger patty with the shredded lettuce, chopped onion, grated cheese, the au jus gravy and all the trimmings. And it's happening to me! I feel wonderful. *I love you, Graciela, I love you, pretty baby...*

"My God, Jerz," I whispered to myself as I gazed at this adorable creature with her big muscular legs and luminous brown eyes, "Is this the woman you're going to be holding in your arms in a few moments?"

When the coast seemed clear, Graciela and I got together in the can. She licked my face frantically and slid her warm tongue into my throat. I jerked her bra up. She yanked my pants down. Then she planted one foot on the toilet seat.

"I wanted to be with you earlier," she whispers, breathing warmly into my mouth, "but I had to chop the onions."

We're kissing and kissing. There are bits of raw onion in her hair. I'm trying to get it in, but the angle is wrong. I've got one foot in the toilet now. Water is pouring into my shoe. Suddenly Graciela lost her balance and grabbed the chain and pulled the water tank off the wall. I felt myself falling. We both hit the deck, and porcelain shattered around us. Jagged gleaming fragments were everywhere. Water spurted on us from above. We were drenched. I didn't know what to do. There was no question of finishing our business. Iron Mike was practically at the door, we were certain of it. Even with his hearing aid turned down to zero he'd had to have heard that racket. The next day Graciela didn't come to work. I never saw her again.

I managed to smooth things over with Mike. But time was growing short for me. Serafina was the next girl to arrive. She had a harelip, but aside from that she was a knockout. A girl with a little defect like that can drive you crazy. I whispered her name to myself, "Serafina, Serafina," while I peeled the spuds. But this time Mike was watching me. And I mean closely. He was wise to my tricks. It was time to pack my traps and skedaddle. I didn't dare tell him I was quitting, so I simply didn't come in to work one day, and thereafter I avoided the 900 block of Broadway.

One thing about Mike: he was a good cook. The cabbage soup (chopped onions, chopped cabbage, caraway seeds) was terrific. I ate well for three weeks; I'll say that.

9

PABLITO POPPED UP SUDDENLY. How he managed to find me I don't know, but I was glad to see him. He'd put a little money together and he was ready for the trip to the migrant labor camp. Bobbo had promised to loan me his van, but we'd been out of touch for some time. I didn't need to go to Bobbo's for the dog food dinners because Jack had also returned and I was eating steak three times a week, thanks to Jack's five-finger discount.

Jack was beside himself on the day that Pablito turned up at Boyle Heights. He claimed that he'd found Tony playing the piano in the lobby at the Westin Bonaventure Hotel downtown and that the Big Guy was hooked up with a Hollywood director who was going to make a kick-ass movie about his life. I didn't believe a word of it, of course, but I liked the way Jack blended fantasy and reality, as if he were mixing batter for a cake. It was obvious that he didn't know what was real and what wasn't, and didn't give a damn.

We ate dinner and sat around the campfire, Jack and Pablito and I, and then we bunked outside, under the stars. It was June or July and the weather was warm. Before we went to sleep Jack told us the story about Tony.

"Tony looked good, I mean he looked good, but his

clothes were ratty, you know? I mean, he'd been sleeping out and shit. But when he sat down at that piano. Jesus! Two security guards were walking up to him, but when he started tickling those keys, tears started streaming down their faces. Everybody was crowding around. The people loved him. We had a drink at the bar between sets. They were going to throw me out, but Tony said, '*Give this man a drink! This man is with me! Give him whatever he wants!*' There was a reporter there and he wrote down everything. I met the director, too. He said they were going to shoot some of the film at Tony's villa in Tuscany. And get this. Who do you suppose is gonna play Tony? Go ahead, take a guess. *Jeremy Irons*, man! Jeremy Irons! Is Jeremy Irons Tony or what? Earlier on they were talking about Gérard Depardieu. But he's too...too... Don't get me wrong, Gérard Depardieu is a great actor! But he's too... But, hey, Jeremy Irons, man. We're talking about a kick-ass movie here. *The Kid's Last Fight*, that's the title. The director said it's going to be a film about redemption...a tribute to the human spirit. Those were his exact words. And the reporter wrote it down."

"Where's Tony now?" I ventured. "I'd like to see him again."

Jack sat up and blew his nose on his sleeve. "Studio City, Pacific Palisades. I'm not sure. He went home with the director. They have a lot to talk about. He'll be in touch. He'll be in touch, don't worry."

Tony was rapidly passing into myth, like Paul Bunyan or Pecos Bill, thanks to Jack's tireless efforts. It's true that when I first met Tony our feet were planted smack dab in the medieval squalor of Fifth Street, but the second meeting was in front of Bullocks Wilshire, and now, as Jack wove his web of dreams, I began to associate the Big Guy with the faded elegance of Wilshire Boulevard, with the faded glory of Hollywood's Golden Age. He was Saturday's Hero, Tony, a high wire walker, he was the Man on the Flying Trapeze, the Last of the Mohicans, a gorgeous moth consumed by a flame, he was a fallen angel fluttering silently to earth under the Klieg lights.

I realized that Pablito had understood very little of what Jack had said but I didn't bother running it down for him because I knew his mind was fixed on his wife and child and the trip to McGonigle Canyon. The last thing I heard as I drifted off to sleep was Pablito saying his prayers:

"*Santa Maria, Madre de Dios, ruega por nosotros…*"

The next day it was over to Bobbo's to pick up the van. Pablito wanted to pay me for the trip but I told him nothing doing, you can just pay for the gas. Before we left I had to drive Bobbo to Uncle Barney's where the silverfish roam, and then, after a brief hello and goodbye to Moms, we were on our way.

Pablito made the trip in the back, rolled up in a rug with cardboard boxes piled on top of him. We had to be careful. There was a checkpoint at San Oenofre. But he was in great spirits, singing all the way.

"*Start spreading the news, I'm leaving today…* The city that never sleeps, right, Jersee? Is that what it means? Open *dia y noche?*"

"Yup! twenty-four-seven!"

"*Está muy lejos?*"

"Yeah, very far."

"More far than San Diego?"

"Yes, four thousand kilometers, *mas o menos.*"

"*Bistek?* They eat *bistek* every day?"

"Every day! And twice on Sundays."

"*These vagabond shoes…* What does it mean, 'vagabond shoes?' "

"It means shoes that never stop walking, no matter what."

Pablito had come through the Cloaca of the World, the Nogales Wash, a sewer pipe connecting Mexico with the US. He'd swum in raw sewage to get here. Human excrement, rats, La Migra: nothing could stop him; nothing could dim his dream of a better life.

"In New York they ride horses, the police. It is true, yes?"

"Horses? Yes, it's true, my friend. White horses. And the cops have plumed helmets. They canter through the streets on white horses, Arabian stallions with plaited manes, *clippity-clop, clippity-clop.* You should hear the trumpets! And girls, beautiful girls with flowers in their hair playing lutes and tambourines and harps and timbrels and leading leopards and cheetahs on leashes. And midgets turning somersaults, and peacocks, gorgeous peacocks with green and gold feathers! *Clippity-clop, clippity-clop!* You see them everywhere, 42nd Street, Broadway, Times Square..."

Pablito! Pablito was the archetypal American immigrant, fresh from Ellis Island, a man following his star from rags to riches, the American Dream or bust. That was my Pablito. He was Papa Di Nucci, the pushcart man who opens a nationwide chain of pizza parlors. He was the Great Gatsby, Andrew Carnegie, Don Vito Corleone. *Give me your huddled masses yearning to breathe free!*

It was late afternoon by the time we got to Rancho Peñasquitos. We parked near some pink tract houses with red tile roofs and plunged quickly into the tangled underbrush of a steep canyon, lugging some bags of groceries we'd brought along.

The migrants were a ragged lot, about eight of them, huddled around an open fire, roasting pepitas on a flattened sheet of tin. There was a hut made out of cardboard, chicken wire and black plastic. They were understandably leery of me, so Pablito walked up on them and they had a little palaver.

I sat down on a rotting log. A lizard darted out and perched on a fallen leaf, motionless, pretending he didn't exist. Then a whole flock of the sweetest little birds suddenly descended and disappeared into a bush. You could hear them inside the bush, flitting from twig to twig, chirping and peeping like mad, but you couldn't see them.

Pablito returned and the birds flew away all at once, a dense noisy cloud of flapping wings. Pablito's wife and child were in another camp, he informed me, deeper in the canyon and some miles distant. It was already getting dark—too late in the day to start out now. I was invited to dinner, he said. I figured they didn't need another mouth to feed but Pablito insisted, so we walked down to the camp.

After we'd eaten, the sky suddenly erupted, spewing out fiery orange pinwheels and blue spider stars. It must have been the Fourth of July. I hadn't been keeping close track of the months or days. The fireworks went on and on. Everyone was in a festive mood. A young girl came up to us, Ysela. She was dying to tell us a story, so we said okay. We sat down on a log. Ysela and her little sister Rosita had gone up to the tract homes that border the canyon. They were going to beg for work or food. They went to a house with a red tile roof.

"The house of the gringos is very big, and very beautiful."

"Okay."

"We ring the bell."

"It was you and Rosita?"

"Yes. *Rosita y yo.*"

"You rang the bell."

"*Sí.*"

"And so?"

"*No están.* Nobody."

"Nobody home?"

"*Nadie! No hay nadie!*"

"*Y entonces? Qué pasó?*"

"Oh, Pablito, we go inside."

"*No me digas!*"

"You mean you…"

"Yeah, we went inside."

"*Hijole!*"

"Was it a nice place?"

"*Claro!* So big. So beautiful! I cannot believe it. You should see Rosita's eyes!"

"Ha, ha! So what happened then?"

"They have a swimming pool in the bathroom."

"*Mentirosa!* You lie."

"No, Pablito! *De veras!* I'm telling you the truth, man! *Es la pura verdad!*"

"You mean a Jacuzzi?"

"*Un Jacuzzi, si, Jersee.* We take a bath."

"You took a bath? Oh, my God, this is beautiful. So you were Queen for a Day!"

"Queen for a Day? I don't understand."

"Never mind. What about food? Did you—"

"*Si! Si!* I open the—*como se llama?*"

"The refrigerator?"

"*Si! Si!* The refrigerator."

"And?"

"*Ay, mi madre,* the food!"

"*Digame!* Tell me, Ysela! The food! Tell me about the food!"

"Oh, Pablito! *Hay pollo y carne y frutas de toda clase.*"

"Watermelon?"

"Yes, watermelon, and grapes, and apples and strawberries!"

"*Que suave!*"

"And ham and eggs and *salchichón.*"

"*Bistek?*"

"*Si, bistek!*"

"*No me digas?*"

"Cheese, Ysela? Swiss cheese, by any chance? Gruyère? Jarlsberg?"

"*Si! Si,* cheese, *Jersee. De toda clase.* And milk, juice, ice cream, pudding…"

"What does it mean, 'pudding'?"

"Pudding, *postre, flan!*"

"*Valgame Dios!*"

"So what happened then? Did you eat?"

"*Sí!* We eat, we drink!"

"What did you…?"

"Oh, chicken, rice, *rosbif*, watermelon, ice cream. Rosita like very much the *rosbif*."

"*Y entonces?* What's happen then?"

"We go upstairs."

"You went upstairs? To the bedroom?"

"Yes. It is very big, the bed. We take a siesta."

"What about the people? Did they come back?"

"*Los gringos?* No. We sleep all night. *Toda la noche.* In the morning I cook breakfast, *huevos revueltos*. We watch TV. I turn on *el aire*."

"You mean they had air conditioning?"

"Yes. I like very much *el aire*."

"So the people…did they ever come back?"

"*Los gringos? Sí, pero más adelante.*"

"You mean later? Later they came back?"

"Yes. *En la tarde.* We hear a car. We look out the window. They are here, *los gringos*."

"You were escared?"

"*Claro!*"

"What did you do?"

"We run, man! We run. We are laughing…"

10

DANIRA OPERATED A FOOD BANK ON SIXTH.
You go in with your hat in your hand, there's a brief
interview, and they give you a bag full of cans of Dinty
Moore Corned Beef hash, B&M Baked Beans, Little
Debbie Honey Buns and Marshmallow Pies. And Top
Ramen, and so on. It was a pretty good deal. A person gets
damned sick of Top Ramen, but it fills you up. My
interview with Danira went well and we seemed to hit it
off. I even thought at the time that there was some
chemistry, and later this instinct of mine proved to be true.
She said I could make ten bucks now and then sorting out
the food donations. She'd get in a whole truckload of
canned goods, noodles, rice, beans and candy, and my job
was to sort through everything, organize it, get rid of the
severely dented and bloated cans, and in the process I was
free to take anything I wanted.

It's amazing the stuff rich folks give away. Tuna,
salmon, Portuguese sardines, snow crab, lobster bisque,
white asparagus spears, blackberry jam. The canned hams
were wonderful, and I adored the smoked oysters and the
lobster bisque. Living well is the best revenge, as they say.
And I threw out can after can of Chef Boyardee Spaghetti,
without a second thought. Nobody should have to eat that

crap. She'd pay me out of her pocket, Danira. I didn't mind the low wages, not with all the freebies. Plus I knew perfectly well that social workers don't make all that much.

Then things started heating up between Danira and me. Danira lived on Mariposa Street—"Butterfly Street"—a few blocks west of Bullocks Wilshire. Whenever I'd go to see Danira I could be reasonably sure that I was going to wind up holding some sailor's pants. I was one of many men Danira held in thrall.

It's true that we didn't have a lot in common. We talked about the movies and I told her that I was crazy about the gangster films, particularly *Goodfellas* and the Al Pacino films, the suitcases full of money and all that. Danira was into horror films, 'intelligent' horror films. She'd seen *Jacob's Ladder* fifteen times. But we both liked to drink. Danira was a juicer. She had to be pretty well spifficated before we got down to the lovey dovey stuff. We drank mostly the jug wines, tokay and muscatel. They say sex is like riding a bicycle, that you never forget how, but I was often so drunk that I couldn't find the handlebars.

Then, too, I no longer knew how to treat a woman. I'd been living in the shadows too long.

The food bank was terrific, but the romance part of it quickly went in the toilet. I know now what I did wrong. I mismanaged the whole affair. Because you have to go about things the right way when it comes to the cuties. *First you get the money, then you get the power, and then you get the woman.* Since I didn't have the money, I tried to cut to the chase. Just, 'get the woman.' All wrong. You can't do it that way. I violated the Pacino Principle, and I paid the price.

I'm not saying we didn't have some good times. Neither Danira nor I had a car, but we didn't consider that an imposition. If she had a day off we'd catch the #21 up Wilshire to Fairfax after spending the morning in bed, and then the #217 to Canter's Deli for pastrami sandwiches and a few glasses of wine, followed by a leisurely stroll along Melrose, then back to Wilshire, the Tar Pits—in the center of the world's most modern city, a primordial sink, fathomless, suppurating—and then, if it happened to be a free Tuesday, we'd hit the Page Museum to gawk at the four hundred and four dire wolf skulls tacked up on the wall. Or we'd go to the Egyptian Theater for a vintage movie and we'd smuggle in our wine in plastic bottles. Danira was drinking hard every day, enough wine to float a battleship, and it was tearing her up inside, chronic gastritis, bleeding hemorrhoids, the works. Her liver must have been tougher than shoe leather.

"Wine is life!" she'd often say to me. "You know how it is in France, Jerz. You've been to Paris, right? Everybody in France drinks wine with meals, children included, and they'll send kids to the corner grocery store for a bottle of wine and nobody thinks anything of it. The French have a high fat saturated diet and yet they have fewer heart attacks than anybody. Why do you think that is, Jerzy? *Red wine!* Wine contains flavonoids and tannins that help to prevent cardiovascular disease. It's common knowledge. And red wine prevents kidney stones. It's even been said that wine was the primary agent for the development of Western civilization! I mean, in ancient Rome everybody drank wine, from the lowest slave right up to the patricians…"

When Danira's favorite sailor boy blew into town, the bosun's mate from the USS John C. Stennis, I knew my goose was cooked. You talk about handsome! The teeth on this guy! Like pearls, Mikimoto pearls. What could I do? This guy was a fucking war hero and here I was, second cousin to Joe Shit the Ragman. What chance did I have? It's in their genes, the cuties. The Sailor and the Girl: they're an archetypal pair, like Cupid and Psyche.

I had a sailor suit once, when I was five or six years old. There was a framed photograph on the mantle, I remember, of me in my sailor suit. Clearly, that was my destiny, to be a sailor. But I outran it, I outran my destiny,

I shrugged it off, stupidly, stupidly. My God, when I think of it, the life that could have been mine. A girl in every port! These are the things you think about when you're sleeping under a bridge and a horde of rabid hyenas are nibbling at your toes.

The thing with Danira was on and off, but the job at the food bank was great. There was plenty to eat and I had enough money for coffee. I'd take a break and go for a walk. I loved sitting in California Plaza with the sun-warmed granite under my ass and a hot Pasqua cafe latte fortissimo in my hand, gazing up at the glass towers reflecting each other, the limpid, aqueous light bouncing from mirror to mirror, everything tenuous, shaky, evanescent.

Before long I brought Jack in on the deal. Then Mrs. Angarola joined us, a friend of Danira's, "Mrs. Egg Roll." She was pudgy-pretty and had a gold tooth in front. We called Mrs. Angarola Mrs. Egg Roll because she was a friend of the owner of a Chinese restaurant and he gave her whatever he was going to toss out that day. She'd go to the back doors of supermarkets too, and pick up discarded vegetables. She'd bring everything back to the food bank, and we'd trim the vegetables and make up little care packages and hand them out to the Raggedy Anns and Raggedy Andys in the streets. It was surprising how many of them would offer some change—even a dollar or two. If they wanted to pay us something, we accepted, but we never pressed them.

It was beautiful. We were eating kung pao chicken every day, and moo shi pork and Peking duck. I had a sense that Mrs. Egg Roll was sweet on me, too. One day at the food bank when Danira wasn't around we were sorting through the cans and I put my arm around her. I wasn't intending to sex her up or anything like that. I just wanted to see what she'd do. She started to kiss me, but suddenly Danira walked in and the moment was lost, which was probably just as well. Looking back, I think maybe Mrs.

Egg Roll simply felt sorry for me. She knew perfectly well that Danira was a sailor's girl at heart and that she was just keeping me around to blow up her tires.

Danira was working as a phone sex operator in her off time. She didn't make any secret of it. I'd go to visit her in the boiler room. Sometimes Jack went with me. Danira was the only halfway decent looking girl, but they were all very congenial. In between calls they'd talk about the usual stuff: kids, boyfriends, bargains. They'd send Jack and me out for pizza when lunchtime came around. We'd go over to LaMonica's, where Jimmy D and I used to hang out.

Danira really got the guys going with that little-girl voice of hers. You could tell she loved performing. It struck me funny how Danira could be so sexy on the phone, loose as a goose up there, and she wasn't at all drunk. Or I should say she was only slightly drunk, because she always kept a little buzz. And yet, when it came down to the real thing, she had to be completely blotto. I always thought that maybe the phone sex was a safe way to act out her fantasies, that maybe she was getting off as much as the guys who called in were.

Danira's co-worker Maxine had a husky, sultry voice. Maxine was a fat girl with a body like a blimp and a little garden of angry red pimples on her forehead. She told us she'd been getting a shitload of calls from Auburn University.

"Them Alabama boys is just like rabbits," she said. "They'll squirt in five minutes. I can do six or seven in an hour. It's the same with the boys from Ole Miss. Must be something in the water down there. Or it could be the collard greens. Or ham hocks, or grits, or corn pone. I mean, they say you are what you eat. If that's true, then them southern boys must be eating rabbit stew twenty-seven."

Jack and I would usually skim off some change when we went for the pizza and we'd have a few beers and talk about Danira. We both knew she was going to dump me. I mean, Jack knew a sailor's girl when he saw one. He tried to his best console me: "That's the way it is with these women. I went through the same thing with Francine. It's like they've got a golf bag full of clubs, only the clubs are cocks. They got the #9 iron, the #4 wood, the putter, and so on. So here she is in the rough on the 14th hole and she says, I guess I'll use the #7 iron. So she calls up the #7 iron—that's Joe. That's Joe's wiener, is what I mean to say. Joe is a penis with a man attached to it. Then a little bit later it's the #2 iron or the #3 iron or the #4 wood, and that's Bob or Eddie or Floyd. That's all these guys are to her—dicks with men attached to them, clubs in a golf bag. Or you might say she's got a quiver full of arrows, and it's just a question of which arrow she wants to shoot up her twat at that particular moment. Let's see, what kind of a wiener do I feel like today? Turkey sausage? Polska kielbasa? Joe? Eddie? Floyd? Big Frankie from Fresno?"

"You know how it is, then."

"Yeah, definitely. I used to caddy."

"No, I mean the other thing, the girl thing."

"Shit yes! Like I said, I've been through it, man. Francine! She put me through the wringer. With Francine I was always the last club to be selected, the last arrow in the quiver. After Mike and Joe and Eddie and Floyd and Big Frankie from Fresno had gone ahead and got her juiced up pretty good, she'd reach for the putter. Picture it, bro, she's on the green now, serene as a daisy with about twenty-seven orgasms under her belt. Now, she just wants to put the finishing touches on things. That's where I come in, see? That's the way it was with Francine. The only difference between me and her vibrator, as far as Francine was concerned, was that with me she didn't have to replace the batteries."

All this was before Danira's sailor lad with the pearl-handled teeth showed up. His aircraft carrier came into Coronado after six months in the Persian Gulf. They docked at North Island before going up to Bremerton and disgorged some five thousand randy deck apes, loaded with money and sperm, and the cuties went wild. It was mob estrus from Pico Rivera to San Ysidro, frantic girls conga dancing in the streets, hordes of them, and Danira, of course, was swept up in this mad mating frenzy, her hormones tweaked beyond reason. A guy like me, what could I do? The sailor always gets the girl.

11

I BEGAN DOING SOME FREELANCE PLUMBING
with a Yugoslavian I met one night at Mohammed's Pizza
Parlor on Sixth, right behind the Wilshire Royale Hotel. I
was living in Lafayette Park at the time. It was a Friday
night and I was juggling the proprietor's baby, little Yasin,
and drinking a forty-ounce King Cobra I'd bought at Big 6
Market just across the street, when this jamoke—whiskey
nose, frizzy white hair, enormous bloodshot Byzantine
eyes—started talking to me.

"You must be the guy from New York. Mohammed's
told me about you. Mind if I sit down? My name is
Vjonovich. George Vjonovich."

"Pleased to meet you."

"You down on your luck?"

"Close to it."

"Want to meet a rich woman?"

"Who doesn't?"

"You're not a bad looking guy. Can you dance?"

"Sure."

"Good. I know this place in Beverly Hills. A lot of rich
skirts go there. All you have to do is dance with them.
They've got one of those big mirror-ball things that spins
around and throws spots of light on the dance floor. They

play the old songs, exclusively. The slow stuff. You know? It's real dark in there, and once you've had a few drinks...well, I'm sure you'll have no trouble at all fooling yourself into believing that the woman you're holding in your arms is young and attractive."

Fatima brought out my pizza and took the baby from me. I asked Vjonovich if he wanted to join me.

"I already ate," he said. "Go ahead, enjoy your pizza." He pulled a flat bottle of Seagram's Seven out of his coat pocket and laced his coffee. "Think you'd be interested?"

"Beverly Hills? Sure."

"Where are you parked?"

"I don't have a car."

"Oh... Well, we'll make it some other time, then."

"What do you do, George?"

"What do you mean?"

"I mean for a living."

"I'm a plumber."

"Need a helper?"

"Maybe. Let me see your hands. Good. Meet me at La Pachanga tomorrow morning at nine o'clock."

So it began, the plumbing venture. We'd meet each morning at La Pachanga, up past the park, west of Koreatown, a hole in the wall in the middle of Little Central America. This Vjonovich liked to hoist a few before getting down to business. By the time we'd get around to tackling the job, we were usually half in the bag. Vjonovich had lost his driver's license on a DUI charge and his truck had been impounded, so we'd travel to the jobs by bus. Strange guy, George Vjonovich. A suicidal drinker. Some of the tools in that canvas bag he carried were mighty suspicious. Pry bars and sharpened screwdrivers. He carried a gun, too. It was a Ceska Zbrojovka Model 75. He always seemed to have money in his pocket. I began to wonder if he wasn't a burglar. The gun made me nervous. But he bought me breakfast and beers and I kept hanging on.

To make it brief, one afternoon Vjonovich was picked up on a public drunk charge and the cops found the gun. Vjonovich went to the slam, and I ended up inheriting his plumbing tools.

Al "Hoffy" Hoffmeyer was from the South, Greensboro, and he was what you might call a bad apple, the kind that has it in him—the desire, if not the ability—to spoil the whole barrel. He had a fatalistic air about him. I mean, Hoffy *wanted* things to go badly. I met Hoffy at the pizza dive. We fell in together right away. It was one of those things, two desperadoes recognized each other, I guess. Hoffy was basically a career dishwasher, and he'd worked for Xerox, too, as a sales rep. He didn't appear to be homeless, but he seemed to have a lot of time on his hands. A young guy, he'd been a high school baseball player and then a soldier. He'd done some time too, I learned later on, for armed robbery, or so he said, but I never believed that part of it. Hoffy didn't have the balls to do armed robbery. He might have knocked over a gumball machine, something like that. Hoffy was a dreamer. Always a pie in the sky. Hoffy had so many pies in his sky that you couldn't get a cloud in edgewise. He dreamed of some distant paradise—Zihuatanejo, Sri Lanka, Mumbai—where all his problems would go away and everything would be different. He talked incessantly about joining the Pygmies of the Ituri Forest and mining for diamonds in the green hell of the Mato Grosso. We'd meet at Mohammed's, jaw about Mumbai and Mexico and Belize and get blitzed on King Cobra. After we got to know each other better, I learned that he actually was homeless, living in his car, so I'd take him by Danira's food bank so he could stock up. We'd hang out at the bar of the Wilshire Royale Hotel, too, whenever we had any money.

Anyway, after Vjonovich got pinched, I got in touch with Hoffy—because he had a car—and took him in as my partner.

At first we made our contacts in bars. We relied on

bravado and my very slight technical knowledge. Before long we landed several clients among Hoffy's friends who worked here and there in offices around the city. It was a sweet deal. They'd invite us to dinner. To them, I suppose, we were interesting characters. They led humdrum lives.

Starting from mid-Wilshire, Hoffy and I worked our way across Los Angeles, leaving a trail of botched jobs and scarred woodwork. Occasionally we'd screw up a job so bad that we panicked and simply got the hell out of there. I'd bust a wrong joint. I had a proclivity for that. Water squirting every whichway. Or I'd strip the threads. A hell of a mess. Always too heavy-handed!

Hoffy, especially, had no mechanical ability, nor, for that matter, the slightest desire to apply himself. While I was hacking and sweating with my hammers and wrenches and things, Hoffy would wander freely through the house, smoking joints and swigging out of a bottle of wine. Of course we saw to it that we did our 'work' while our clients were off at their jobs.

Hoffy thought nothing of making himself a sandwich; always a whopper, too. Salami, liverwurst, sardines, onions, pickles, several kinds of cheese, whatever the refrigerator had to offer. Nothing was too good for him! He'd sit at the kitchen table watching me, or worse, he'd perch on the commode, munching a sardine sandwich and smacking his lips like a baboon while I wrestled with a clogged bathtub drain. And plying me with questions, with conundrums, you might even say. It was the *idea* of plumbing that interested him, the philosophy of plumbing, if there is such a thing. To top it off, he was terribly light-fingered. Rings, watches, small change. He raided the medicine chests, too. Drugs, anything he could touch.

Finally, I called a halt to the operation. It was getting too hot. I made the decision without consulting Hoffy. And just to be sure I wouldn't be tempted to go back into the venture, I took a bus to Echo Park and dumped the canvas bag of plumbing tools into the drink. *Ya se acabó!*

That was the end of it. Plumbing is like dentistry or tree surgery. You have to have a feel for it. Some's got it, and some don't.

After that I lost track of Hoffy for several months, which was probably just as well. I thought he might have been pinched on a parole violation. By now I was living back over in Boyle Heights. Then one fine spring day I ran into Hoffy at California Plaza and he presented me with an astonishing bit of news: he'd decided to do something with his life. We figured a few beers were in order, so we went to Phillipe's on the edge of Chinatown, one of my favorite haunts (memories of Ashlee), sawdust on the floor, roomy, no television, excellent food, fair prices, pretty waitresses.

Hoffy had a plan. He wanted to go to Greensboro, North Carolina, his hometown, and try out as an outfielder with the Greensboro Grasshoppers, a Class A baseball team in the South Atlantic League. He'd been busting suds at Clifton's, I learned, had saved some money, fixed up the car, a beat-up old Trans Am, and he'd taken out a loan, so he said, to finance the venture. He wanted me to go along. My role would be to hit him flies and grounders, help him get into shape, bolster his confidence, and act as his trainer, sort of. My expenses would be paid. That was the deal.

"What the hell, Jerz, you need to get out of LA. A change of pace will do you good. Come on, what do you say?"

I said yes, so we climbed into that battered purple Trans Am, a white-trash car if there ever was one. I admit that I didn't have much confidence in Hoffy's plan. I was going along primarily because I didn't have anything better to do. I tried to hide my feelings from Hoffy so as not to queer the deal but my real opinion, my honest opinion, was that the venture was shot in the ass from the word go.

The engine was chugging. Hoffy kept socking his fist into the oiled pocket of his Willie Mays centerfielder's mitt. *Eldon Aldreau Hoffmeyer, little jive nobody!* Hoffy thought small. When he saw a big hotel like the Hilton or even the Wilshire Royale, he thought immediately of the bellhops and elevator operators, what their hours were, how much they made, and whether they humped the maids in the dirty clothes hamper, and so on, yet he envisioned himself in a vague sort of way as someday 'making it big'.

"I can do it! I mean that. Come on, Jerz, don't be so damned *negative!* I mean it! I'm telling you, I really mean it!"

He did. Mean it, I mean. He was serious. He was all fired up. *Spring.* It had Hoffy by the throat. He had baseball fever.

We drove to Greensboro and got a room on Hydrangea Street near Hoffy's old neighborhood. The place was an ancient plantation-style boarding house with white pillars and soft beds and heavenly home-cooked meals.

Baseball players! After supper, Hoffy and I would play catch on the boarding house lawn, impressing (we thought) the southern belles who sat rocking on the rickety wooden porch among fragrant filigrees of jasmine and dazzling twinkles of antebellum chandeliers emanating from the hallway. And the lawn sprinklers whirling, katydids serenading, the porch swing creaking, a screen door slamming down the block, the honeysuckles spitting dew like fountain cupids. So lush, the South. Sometimes Hoffy would offer the girls a stick of Beechnut gum. Such innocence! When it got too dark to see the ball, we'd walk to Roberts Grocery Market for an Orange Crush out of the beat-up old cooler. Hoffy insisted that there be no drinking until the tryouts were over. Actually, I didn't need a drink. I felt wonderful with all that fresh air and the daily workouts and the terrific meals. The clean life! I must have taken dozens of showers.

There were two cooks at the boarding house, Bessie Mae Brown and Johnnie Mae Wright. Bessie Mae Brown was big, so big that she gave birth to twins and was back at work the next day and nobody even knew she was pregnant. Johnnie Mae Wright, on the other hand, was thin, bone thin. The two ladies alternated days. Mornings I'd venture into the kitchen. I loved to watch Bessie Mae Brown cook breakfast in the big iron skillet. The bacon was the thick kind, slab bacon; and then she'd cook the eggs, sunny side up, over medium, any way you wanted, in the hot bacon grease. Even if you didn't go back to the kitchen, you could tell who was cooking that day by the biscuits. Bessie Mae Brown's biscuits were light and fluffy, and poked full of butter and honey there was nothing better. But Johnnie Mae Wright's biscuits were like lumps of lead. You'd try to float them in the gravy and they sank like rocks.

Every afternoon Hoffy and I played sandlot ball in a field near a laundry. It was a regular ballpark with a dirt infield, bleachers and a scoreboard topped with a Bardahl sign in deep centerfield perched on the edge of a Piggly Wiggly parking lot. Across the street was an old folks' home, painted bright yellow, pink and blue, like an Easter egg. Under enormous live oaks dripping with Spanish moss, the oldsters gamboled on the green, some of them in speedy motorized wheelchairs and swinging croquet mallets. *The golden years.* Twin plumes of smoke belched from the stacks of the laundry, and a block down the street, just before the railroad tracks, was a Tastee Freez. The ballplayers were young mechanics, factory workers or farm kids, many of them still in high school. Everybody was getting ready for the tryouts, coming up in two weeks.

The opposing team had a whirlwind of a pitcher, Porky Heissert, a stocky young redneck who pitched every other game. Porky Heissert had a fastball that came up hissing, and a foot in front of the plate it veered and hopped like a Mexican jumping bean. You could hear him grunting from the sidelines when he pumped the ball up there. His motion threw him off to the side of the mound, and then he did a quick hop-jig-jump into position with his glove flung in front of him. *Porky Heissert, the Human Catapult.* He had a hook that fell off the table. Sometimes he took a little off the hook and it came up mean and sharp, then dived, wobbling like a crippled minnow. Hoffy couldn't hit Porky Heissert, and I realized then, at the beginning of the venture—as Hoffy himself must have realized—that he would never be able to stand up to Class A pitching when the tryouts rolled around.

It was at this juncture that Hoffy revealed to me that he had a double purpose in returning to Greensboro. The first was the baseball tryouts. The second was Flora Ann Roberts, a girl from his high school days. Her father owned the corner grocery store in Hoffy's old neighborhood, Roberts Grocery Market. Flora Ann Roberts—I want to make this crystal clear from the start—was Hoffy's karmic apparition, not mine. Hoffy had any number of these half-remembered *femmes fatales* floating around in his past. It was a past that Hoffy carried with him like a mailman lugging a sack bursting with fat letters that are begging to be ripped open and read, and this burden of his unlived lives with these many half-forgotten, and in some cases perhaps only half-real, women was driving him down, buckling his knees, grinding his nose into the ruts of a road sprinkled with nostalgia and moon dust. It was a road that led backward, not forward.

As a kid, Hoffy had bought penny candy at Roberts Grocery Market. Later he'd bagged groceries there, following his senior year in high school, when he was in love, unrequitedly, with Flora Ann. It had been exactly twelve years since his thwarted love affair with Flora Ann, and now he was attempting to return to the past. *Bottomless pit! Quicksand! Danger!* I tried to sound a warning at the onset, but Hoffy wouldn't listen to me. His ears were filled with the melancholy love songs of the sirens. Flora Ann was still clerking at the store, living in the back with the family and playing fairy godmother to the lot, the mother a cripple, her back twisted like a pretzel, the father a parsimonious piddling storekeeper who on Sundays metamorphosed into a marvelously articulate, seemingly rational Baptist deacon, and the maiden aunt and three certified virginal younger sisters who glowed like sugared gumdrops or uncut opals against a shimmering background of prickly heat and billions of fireflies flirting and looping in a midsummer night's dream.

Hoo, boy...

Flora Ann, now thirty-one, was corresponding with a Navy lieutenant and going to Bible meetings four nights a week at her father's church. There's something extraordinarily attractive about flesh that's ripe and perishing, and I was soon caught up myself in this moony delirium, going to prayer meetings in the fish-box wooden church, holding the maiden aunt's sweaty hand, reading from the Book of Revelation, singing hymns, taking Communion. The atmosphere of the church was close and intense, like the hypersexual ward of a madhouse packed with masturbation fiends secretly twiddling themselves off with bobby pins under stiff white hospital gowns. The frozen smiles, the suppressed titters, the wistful, calf-like glances, the hermetic agonies of unbearable tension, the breathless churchy patter that went on between hymns, the girls in their piously outrageous snaky dresses, reeking with delicious perfume, the beads of sweat falling on the pages of the open hymnals.

It was preposterous! I couldn't take it.

Bubba Morgan lived at the boarding house. He worked as a mechanic at Beanie's Garage near the railroad tracks. Sometimes after practice in the afternoons Hoffy and I would meet Bubba at Tastee Freez, just a block from Beanie's. We'd munch ice cream cones and watch the freights go by. I liked Bubba at first. But then it began to pall. In the beginning I naïvely imagined that Bubba was nature's priest, the natural man that Hoffy dreamed of being. But Bubba didn't talk the way I wanted him to talk. Each time he opened his mouth, the perfect untutored diction of the poetic Deep South Robin Hood fled before the eight-cylinder dual-carbureted metric scheme of iambic gasp and wheeze. Bubba's other subject, besides cars, was girls. He liked to do it up the ass. He claimed the honeys were wild about it, especially the Bible-thumpers. He was forever talking about reaming out their intake manifolds, giving them a lube job and packing their hockey boxes with Neo Cambered axle grease.

"I'll see y'all at Tastee Freez!" That's the way Bubba always said goodbye.

At Flora Ann's, the glowing TV squats in the middle of the lettuce-crate living room. It's like being inside a boxcar. We're drinking Kool-Aid, the slick programs are coming on air, and the younger girls are fingering themselves off under their dresses. Flora Ann's crippled mother, peanut-shaped, perches like a scrawny chicken on the edge of the couch. She cranes her neck, she fluffs out her feathers, she's cackling about a furniture sale at Sears. The Deacon, in his underwear, hunches over the desk. He's tallying up the store receipts. The reason he'd take off his pants was, I guess, so the air could circulate through his crotch. From time to time, as he added up the columns of figures, he'd reach down and flick his balls—*thump*—with his index finger. Apparently, it helped him think.

On top of the TV was a gilt-framed photo of Flora Ann in her pleated cheerleader's skirt and white letter sweater and white plastic boots with bunny puffs, the same photo, smaller size, that Hoffy carried in his wallet. He'd jerked off to it hundreds of times over the years.

At the church, Flora Ann sits half-dozing in her chair, legs crossed, her hands folded over her Bible, a regular candy saint, sweeter than a pecan praline, with—maybe—an enormous tapeworm coiled up in her intestines and snoring away like a papoose. She swings her shank, works the upper thighs; they rub together, her little twitchet's oozing, she's getting it excited. She'll be getting her gun, most likely, between First and Second Corinthians. Meanwhile the worms are burrowing under the skin, making everything itch like crazy. Pinworms, hookworms, long slender ones, biting and chewing, squirming like tiny acrobats, everything infested.

But let's get back to the action on the diamond. For the two-week period I popped up twice, walked once, struck out thirty-four times and hit one home run. There were two men on base when I hit that homer, and it won the game for us. It was the only game we did win. The pitcher was Porky Heissert, the Human Catapult.

Okay, *here I am*, bottom of the ninth, two away, two men on. I squat in the on-deck circle, I knock the dirt out of my spikes. I swing my personal timber, an Adirondack Pedro Guerrero 33.

Batter up!

I step into the box, I dig in, waggle my bat. *Whoosh!* He blew me down with the first pitch. *Gotta keep 'em loose up there!* I get back onto my feet, dust off the seat of my pants. *Ball one.* Okay. Okay. Here comes the pitch. *Oof!* The high hard one, again... I missed by a mile. *One and one.* Okay. One and one. I waggle my bat. Here it comes. *The hook!* He pulled the string on me! *Bastard!* I went fishing! Okay. I step outta the box, tap the dirt out of my spikes. The count is one and two. I dig in at the plate, clamp down on my wad of bubblegum that's like a rock in my cheek. Okay. *Ready.* Next pitch... I don't know what happened. Either Porky Heissert was dreaming about catching a mess of channel cats in the Swanee River or he thought, rightly enough, that I was such a lousy hitter that I couldn't touch him no matter what he served up, but he eased off, a fat melon that split the plate, shoulder high, like a big floating creampuff. *Smack!* The instant I connected, I knew it was gone—up, up, and over the centerfield Bardahl sign and into the Piggly Wiggly parking lot. They didn't even bother looking for the ball.

OF COURSE HOFFY AND I never made it to the tryouts. On the day before the tryouts—it was the day of my homer, in fact—Hoffy and I were hoofing it back to the boarding house after Hoffy'd had a particularly bad day at the plate (grounding into a double play and whiffing three times, once with the bases loaded), and who do we run into but our mechanic pal Bubba, just emerging from Beanie's Garage. Bubba was headed home from work, and he had a mayonnaise jar full of white lightning in his lunch pail. Of course we got drunk, the three of us sitting on a railroad trestle, then, during supper, Hoffy makes a pass at one of the maiden ladies at the boarding house, feeling her buns under the table, and later exposing himself to her on the stairway. I'd gone out for a stroll through the leafy neighborhood, and when I got back I learned what had happened. The maiden lady had filed a complaint, the cops had been there, and Hoffy was a wanted man.

O Darkies, how my heart grows weary!

But wait! Stop the music! That wasn't the end of it. We didn't skip town. Not yet. No, this wasn't the finale. Hoffy still couldn't cut the cord. He simply couldn't leave without having one more go at Flora Ann. So we camped out, in the Trans Am, in the piney woods. It was near the railroad tracks. We drove a long way into the woods so the cops wouldn't spot the car. It was goofy rolling on the soft spongy carpet of pine needles while branches splashed against the windshield.

"Far enough! That's far enough! It's getting soupy!"

"Okay! Okay!"

Hoffy was clinging like a drowning man to the blackened edges of a dream. From the piney woods we could see the ballpark across the railroad tracks, and Tastee Freez and the towering pillars of steam billowing from the twin smokestacks of the laundry. At night under the pine boughs festooned with Spanish moss and Cherokee roses I tossed and turned in my bedroll while freights shuddered by, making the earth tremble. The air was damp and cold, and when the wind shifted I smelled the stink of the pulp mills. *The enemy never sleeps!*

Evenings we went to Flora Ann's for supper, as if nothing had happened. We were still living in the myth of trying out for the team. *Athletes! Baseball players!* It was excruciating, a regular Golgotha. One night Flora Ann played the *John Denver's Greatest Hits* album and we all got dewy-eyed—except for the Deacon, the little church mouse, hunched over his desk in his underwear, scribbling madly, thumping his balls, tallying up the store receipts.

Then came the night when I walked past the bathroom, and the door was ajar, and I saw Flora Ann, sitting on the edge of the tub with her legs apart and her skirt hiked up around her waist. She was diddling herself off with a bobby pin. She had fur right up to her navel. Her belly was one big beard. Staring at that thing, Flora Ann's pussy, something came over me. This was the source of everything, the wellspring of life and misery. *The tuft of hair that made the Buddhas cry!* You came out kicking and screaming, reluctant as hell to leave, and you spent the rest of your life trying to get back in. Exile, refugee, kicked out of paradise, you wander aimlessly, obsessed with the idea of getting back to where you've been. *Keep moving!* That's the litany that rings in your ears. You stumble forward in darkness, little jive nobody, picking your way along the railroad tracks. You put your ear to the ground. The earth trembles.

There'll be a freight along in a minute.

Flora Ann, with her simmering blue eyes, ringed with haunted circles of mascara, Flora Ann, whom I'd christened "The Black Dahlia," Flora Ann, so inviting, so wasted, probably crawling with trichinosis, her full virginal lips smeared with soot and ashes. I smelled the lilies of death. This was the song of the Loreleis. I wanted out. But Hoffy still couldn't let go. He was sinking deeper and deeper into a quagmire of fleshy nostalgia. His umbilical cord was twisted around his neck; he was suffocating.

"Fuck this, Al," I said. "You know what? I was better off in Boyle Heights."

"For God's sake, Jerz!" he howled. "Give me one more day! I had her bra off last night, I swear. The *nipples*... They're hard as nails. And *long*...like little *cocks!*" He hopped from one foot to the other, clenching his fists; he clutched at the air, he ripped a branch off a pine tree, he was almost in tears, he seemed to be praying to me.

"Let me have one more go at her, then we'll get on the road. Don't worry; I'll pay the gas. *One day! One day!* Is that so much to ask?" He smashed his fist against a tree trunk. He dived into a thicket and rolled on the ground, bleeding from a dozen cuts, and roared like a boar hog. "Please, Jerz! One more day! I'll get into her! I know I will!"

Two days later I announced that I'd had enough. It was afternoon. Hoffy was looped on wine. He'd been drinking all day. Now he was talking about breaking into the Class D Alabama-Florida League.

"I'm changing my whole stance, my whole philosophy of hitting. Just meet the ball. Go for the bingle, you know? Little bingle up there, buddy boy! Like Maury Wills! *You remember Maury Wills?*"

Sitting on the pine needles, completely sozzled, he thumbed through a month-old copy of *The Sporting News*.

"Listen to this, Jerz. The Alabama-Florida circuit: Crestview, Donalsonville, Dothan, Fort Walton Beach, Panama City, Palmetto, Sopchoppy, Williston, Two Egg. Those are great towns!"

I handed Hoffy the car keys, which I'd been keeping in anticipation of the big push back to California. Hoffy was a rotten driver, and lazy. I'd figured on doing most of the driving myself.

"Look, Al," I said calmly. "I'll see you in LA."

I shouldered my bedroll and started walking, padding along on the soft pine-needle carpet. I cleared the piney woods, picked my way across the railroad tracks, climbed up into the town and made for the main highway.

Baseball players! *Jesus!*

I didn't know if I'd ever see Hoffy again, and I didn't

care, but three hours later he pulled up alongside me in that beat-up old Trans Am as I trudged grimly forward under the lacy pepper trees, still in the suburbs, sweating like a baggage boy in the sweltering heat.

Near the Tennessee border we parked at a Dairy Queen and Hoffy broke out a shoebox filled with sandwiches and cookies, which he confessed he'd wheedled out of Flora Ann's mother at the kitchen door, just before picking me up on the highway. The severing of the umbilical cord, admittedly one of the most harrowing events in the entire obstacle course, was very difficult for Hoffy. In the center of the human body is a round scar, which everyone has. This is the Serial Number, ID Stamp, symbol of the First Deportation. This is the brand: Exile, Wanderer, Pilgrim. After Genesis, Exodus. You're cut off, kicked out, cast adrift, a fugitive and a vagabond on the earth. We are all refugees, and we have the scar to prove it.

12

I DON'T SAY THE TRIP WAS ENTIRELY WASTED. I mean, that was my thinking once I got back to Boyle Heights. For one thing, I'd gained twenty pounds. I'd shed that lean, hungry look. I could see it in people's eyes. You simply can't let people know how desperate you are. It scares them off. Thanks to Bessie Mae Brown's southern cooking, I'd developed, around my middle, a little cushion of fat, my 'insurance packet', as I thought of it. You might not have a penny to your name, but as long as you have that little cushion of fat, you're ready to rub elbows, *a civilized man!* You hang around hotel lobbies and railroad platforms patting that little cushion of fat, that beautiful insurance packet of yours, with a benevolent, slightly vacant look in your eye—as if you're about to burp—and people say, *yes, wonderful, here's a man who's going places!* And they can't do enough for you. They want to have coffee with you, they'll invite you for a drink; they might even want to talk about the baseball scores. *You're one of them.* But slink around with your tail between your legs and they'll throw beer cans at you. *But once you've got that little cushion, that twenty extra pounds of fat...*

IT WAS A BANNER DAY FOR ME when I met Juan Tomás, and the beginning of a golden period. The meeting took place at the famous Original Tommy's, Beverly and Rampart, where we both had our faces buried in chili cheeseburgers. How we got started talking about Eugene V. Debs I don't know (Eugene V. Debs was the American statesman who spent his life trying to make the poor understand that they were born for something better than slavery and cannon fodder). It was the story of the warden weeping when Debs was released from the federal pen at Atlanta that started things off. That and the chili cheeseburgers. We were both crazy about Tommy's chili cheeseburgers.

Actually, I have Danira to thank for the meeting with Juan Tomás. We'd gone to Tommy's, Danira and I—it was just before we split the blanket—for the chili cheeseburgers, and after we'd plopped down at the counter and ordered, in walks Juan Tomás, who, it turns out, was an old flame of Danira's.

Juan Tomás is a wealthy and cultured Brit with homes in Alicante and Los Angeles. His name is John Thomas Higgins, but he prefers to be called Juan Tomás. At the time, he published an anarchist newspaper in Esperanto, *La Voĉo de l'Popolo*, from his office in Beverly Hills.

I never told Juan Tomás that I was homeless. I was too embarrassed. Right from the beginning he accepted me as an equal. But he knew I was poor, and in order to help me out, and because he apparently valued my input, Juan Tomás asked me if I would act as his psychological counselor for three sessions a week at fifty bucks a pop. He said he had some issues he wanted to work through. I told him that, as a friend, I'd do it for nothing, but he wouldn't hear of it.

Anyway, I became his shrink. So far so good. Juan Tomás is a sparkling conversationalist, and I thoroughly enjoyed the sessions, which were held at his place and usually included a sumptuous lunch or dinner. Then things became more complicated. One of Juan Tomás's anarchist friends asked him to recommend a shrink, and before I knew what had happened, I had two patients, and then several. Since I had no office, I counseled my patients in Juan Tomás's office in Beverly Hills.

I want to make one thing crystal clear before we proceed any further. It was never my intention to hoodwink anyone, or to pass myself off as a psychiatrist in order to bilk unsuspecting clients of their money. Nor did Juan Tomás have any such intention. The whole thing just sort of happened.

Early on, I felt terribly uncomfortable and out of place. I wanted to make a clean breast of things, but I couldn't find a way to bring up the subject with my patients. Besides, they were all crazy about me, right from the get-go. Already I was building up quite a reputation as a healer. I admit it went to my head. But more about that later. Despite the discomfort, it was a golden period. Suddenly I was making money. *Tony Montana, the world is yours!* Actually, I had more money in my pockets than I knew what to do with. I gave it out in the streets to my favorite beggars. And from time to time I'd stay in Motel 6 for a while, in order to freshen up, and I'd stake Jack to a motel stay too, in his own room.

My patients were an interesting lot. Phil was short and wanted to be tall. Jeff was tall, very tall. He wanted to be short, or at least shorter. Mary Ann was a nymphomaniac, or a former nymphomaniac. She wanted to be a man. Damian lived with his mother. He thought he might be gay but wasn't sure.

Phil was my best patient. He was only thirty-three, the age of Christ crucified, but already he was losing his hair. His crown of thorns, as I mentioned, was his diminutive size. He didn't like being a runt, and this perceived defect had colored his whole life. He tried to compensate: bodybuilding, bungee jumping, skydiving. None of it helped, of course.

I wanted to say to him: "Phil, you're a runt. It doesn't matter; believe me. Napoleon was a runt. Charlie Chaplin was a runt. Mahatma Gandhi was a runt. Just be the best runt you can be."

But I didn't say it. I didn't say much of anything. I listened. I let him talk. I let all of them talk. I listened attentively, I asked questions, and I stayed out of it. That was the secret of my popularity. I let them talk and talk and talk. And I listened. And one and all told me: "You know, I feel like I could tell you anything. You're the wisest person I ever met."

It was their own wisdom they were seeing, not mine. I was merely a facilitator. I held the burp bag, and they vomited it all up, everything they hadn't completely digested, everything that was sticking in their craw: their pain, their fears, their longing. I gave them permission to spill it all out, to get everything out on the table where they could see it and deal with it.

Phil had a keen interest in psychology, and he was well informed. One day after the therapy session he suggested that we have a drink. He wanted to go out to a bar, but I had to meet Juan Tomás later on, so I suggested having a drink in the office. I fetched a bottle of mahogany-colored Fondillón from the liquor cabinet, and a few of Juan Tomás's short stubby cigars.

"Doctor Mulvaney—"

"Please. Call me Jerzy. Have a cigar?"

"Jerzy, what do you think of the Behaviorists? Pavlov, for example, or Watson. Or Skinner. What do you think of Skinner?"

"Skinner? He belongs in the laboratory with his rats."

"So you're primarily a psychoanalyst, then."

"Well, not exactly."

"Is your approach along Freudian lines? Or would you call yourself a Jungian psychoanalyst?"

"I wouldn't say that." I was starting to feel confident now. Or maybe it was the wine. "I've been much more influenced by Jung's colleague, Otto Rank."

"Please go on."

"Rank sees neurosis as a transitional phase between the so-called normal man and the artist. This is not to say that every neurotic will blossom into an artist. He doesn't mean that. But what Rank's theory does is take the sting out of being neurotic. Viewed in this context, you see, neurosis is an opportunity for transformation. If you're neurotic, it's because you're supposed to be neurotic, in the same way that a flower has to bud before it blooms. It's an organic process."

"So how much of it is up to us, whether we bloom or not? Are you saying that we have no more choice in the matter than a flower?"

"That's a good question, Phil," Juan Tomás interjected as he stepped briskly into the office and joined us.

And away we went. Free will and destiny, Sartre and Camus, Nietzsche's *Ubermensch*, Romanticism versus Realism, art as politics and politics as art. When the conversation turned to Diego Rivera and art as a function of ideology, Juan Tomás dug out another bottle of the heavenly Alicante Fondillón.

"A favorite of Edmond Dantes, the Count of Monte Cristo," he remarked as he filled our glasses with fragrant wine.

We returned to our discussion of Rivera's murals, which Phil maintained were not art but propaganda since they were harnessed to the Communist ideology. I agreed, but Juan Tomás countered with Rivera's famous Rockefeller Center statement, "All art is propaganda," and that seemed to settle the matter.

"Sartre and Nietzsche both attempted to replace traditional morality with an ethics based on authenticity," Phil said a moment later. "And Sartre talked about 'living an authentic life.' If anyone is living an authentic life, it seems to me that it's you, Jerzy."

"Thank you, Phil. But I…"

"No, really. You're a successful psychiatrist, and a damn good one, I might add. You have the perfect life!"

Fortunately, just at that moment the phone rang in the other room. Juan Tomás vaulted out of his chair and raced to the phone. A moment later he was back.

"It's my fiancée, Nittaya, calling from Bangkok," he explained breathlessly. "You'll have to excuse me."

I stood up quickly, hoping that Phil would take the hint. He did and I was off the hook. But I hardly slept all night. The masquerade would have to end soon, that much was certain. I simply couldn't go on with it.

But as it turned out, I wasn't going to get off that easy. The very next day Belén showed up. Belén from Argentina. She'd been a staunch supporter of Eva Peron before becoming an anarchist. Juan Tomás was ecstatic. We all had dinner together at his home. Juan Tomás loves to cook for people and the presence of an attractive woman sent him into culinary raptures. He fixed his special grilled calamari with saffron rice. After dinner Juan Tomás broke out the Muscatel and the Cuban Puro cigars, and we talked for some time—in Spanish, because Juan Tomás insisted—about Evita and the Peron Regime, embarrassing for me with my crude Mexican Spanish full of English words and border slang. When Juan Tomás excused himself and went to the bathroom, Belén said to me in English: "My God, he hasn't changed a bit. Juan Tomás and his *pernicious* cigars!"

Belén's remark made a strong impression on me. Because 'pernicious' is an unusual word, even for a native speaker, and Belén's English wasn't particularly good. From that moment forward I associated the word 'pernicious' with Belén even though there was no rational or objective reason to do so. It was one of those first impression things.

After Belén had departed I told Juan Tomás about Belén's remark.

"That woman has a nose like a rabbit," he declared,

puffing his pernicious cigar. "Did you notice how she crinkles her nose up as if she's sniffing the air? It's part of her tentativeness, her timidity. She's afraid to venture out of her own briar patch. But you'll find out, when you get her in therapy. You'll need to take a firm hand with her. Well, I don't want to tell you your business."

We finished the bottle of Muscatel and Juan Tomás popped open another one.

"I'll tell you something else," he said, slipping me a salacious wink and lowering his voice to a whisper, "I'll bet she *fucks* like a rabbit, too!"

Juan Tomás was right, as usual. It happened right there in the office, about a week later. I felt awful about having sex with a patient, but there was precious little I could do about it. She climbed up on the desk and opened her legs. The fierce attraction she felt for me came about through transference. That was plain enough to see. It was transference. She wasn't in love with me. And I certainly wasn't in love with her. I kept waiting for counter transference to set in, but it didn't happen.

Belén was the manager of Ferncrest Manor, a retirement home in Hollywood, up near the observatory. It was a wonderful old Victorian house with a gazebo on the rooftop. Sometimes we got together there, in one of the empty rooms or in the linen closet. I loved our sessions in the linen closet because the stacks of neatly-folded starched sheets and the fresh laundry smells seemed to be an assurance that there was at least some vestige of cleanliness and order left in the world.

As time went by I became friendly with several of the guests. There were two maiden ladies, sisters, Dora and Donna. They were senile as parrots. We had wonderful Alice-in-Wonderland conversations with dangling participles and unfinished phrases that simply flitted away on the breeze. I often played cards with the sisters in the evenings, euchre, sitting on the verandah. It was peaceful out there with the lawn sprinklers gently whirling and the sky over Hollywood glowing a dull smog-copper red. I didn't have the remotest idea of how to play euchre and I don't think the sisters knew either. It didn't seem to matter in the least.

Belén had issues with her father. He'd left the family when she was quite young. He kept in touch, but at what, for the young Belén, was an agonizing distance. An anarchist filmmaker and friend of Luis Buñuel, he was in Paris, then in Mexico, Spain, London, what have you, all over the globe. Her early life had been dedicated to winning him back. She failed miserably. Her father ran off with a Parisian strumpet half his age and was never seen again.

Belén did have a nose like a rabbit. Juan Tomás was right about that, too. She was hyper vigilant, very wary, forever sniffing the air, as if on the lookout for predators. She had a deeply ingrained fear of being abandoned. When she was upset her nose twinkled like an angry strawberry. She became very resentful if she thought she was being in the least neglected. Seemingly soft and fluffy as an Easter bunny, she was actually very demanding and possessive. She wanted the last drop of juice, everything. As the weeks went by, I began to feel trapped. I couldn't begin to return her affections with anything like the intensity she desired.

We didn't have a name for Belén's cunt. It wasn't that sort of a relationship, but she did have a very sensitive pubic bone, and this condition led to a nickname of sorts. The problem, she said, was due to chronic bone marrow edema, the result of a sports injury. She'd played soccer, *fútbol*, in Argentina as a young girl. After that first time on top of my desk, we always made love on the couch, usually with her on top. If I got on top, she would caution me not to thrust too hard and bump into her ailing pubic bone:

"No bump-bump!"

Maybe things could have worked out, I often thought, if only our lovemaking could have been freer, more passionate, more violent and unrestrained. But because of

Belén's super-sensitive pubic bone, we had to go at it gingerly, like old folks. Even so, it was frequently exciting right up until the crucial moment, when I would hear her admonishing voice in my ear: "No bump-bump!"

This was the factor that threw cold water on things. We had almost no common interests, it's true, but more than anything else it was the bump-bump business.

For me, the highlight of the Belén period came one night when Juan Tomás invited the two of us to one of his marvelous gourmet dinners. We started with an apéritif, vermouth on the rocks with a twist of lemon. Belén and I sat at the kitchen table watching as Juan Tomás peeled and minced the garlic for the alioli sauce for the *patatas bravas*. What Juan Tomás can do with an ordinary potato is astonishing, as we were soon to discover.

The main dish was to be a paella, he informed us. There were a great many ingredients, so Juan Tomás invited us both to pitch in and help with the preparations. I was allowed to scrub the mussels with a stiff brush. But first we had to fortify ourselves with wine. Juan Tomás poured a fragrant red Monastrell.

"There's nothing quite like a good Monastrell," Juan Tomás said. "Great nose, beautiful bouquet. Wonderful fruit. Can you taste the blackberries? The spices and pepper?"

"Black cherries," Belén whispered. "And flowers…"

The *sofrito* sauce for the paella—olive oil, garlic, red onion, chopped parsley—was bubbling musically on the stove, filling the kitchen with a heavenly aroma. My mussels were simmering in white wine.

Juan Tomás filled our glasses again, and out came the other ingredients for the paella—Roma tomatoes, green peppers, a pork filet, and several good-sized prawns. And, to our surprise, a huge red lobster. Juan Tomás split the lobster lengthwise with a single whack of his cleaver and shucked it out of its shell. Belén was given the job of cutting the succulent pink lobster meat into bite-sized pieces.

More wine, this time a hearty, sweet Muscatel. My head was swimming.

"This won't be a paella, strictly speaking," Juan Tomás told us, carefully arranging his potatoes on a baking tray, "but rather a *fideuà* , which is served with noodles or black rice."

He held up a small bottle of something that looked like soy sauce. "Cuttlefish ink, for the black rice."

After the dinner, and the pernicious cigars, which sent Belén scampering back to her briar patch, Juan Tomás and I settled down for a nice chat.

"What do you think of me, *really*?" Juan Tomás began, as he poured the marvelously aromatic Monastrell.

"Well…" I muttered, momentarily at a loss for words. *Rather direct question, what?*

"No, I mean clinically speaking. Just between us. Therapist and patient. Really, I'd like to know."

"Well, you're an enormously sophisticated man, JT."

"Yes?"

I took a deep breath and plunged in. "Under the bonhomie and the erudition, there's a little ogre who wants to upset the apple cart. This is the archetypal anarchist in you."

"Passive aggressive?"

"Exactly."

"But what's under that? Can you tell me? What is my underlying neurosis?"

"Frankly, JT, I think we're looking at an Oedipal situation."

"You don't say, Old Sport."

"Your lifelong rebellion against all forms of authority stems from the infant's desire to murder the father and possess the mother. This is a gross oversimplification, of course. There's also a need to manipulate others, and to live vicariously through them."

"Are you thinking of our relationship, then? Yours and

mine?"

"Well, I…"

"Come on now, Old Sport, you can speak freely with me. You're my friend as well as my psychotherapist. You're thinking of the Belén business, aren't you? The way I tried to push her on you."

"In another age, JT, you might have been my patron. In a sense, I would have belonged to you. *'As for living, our servants will do that for us!'* Do you remember that phrase?"

"Yes, of course. Villiers, *Axel's Castle*. Well put, Old Sport. You've made an excellent point. I freely admit that I'm a collector of rare specimens. I'm fascinated by the creative mind. I haven't a jot of creativity in me. That's a pity, but it's true. And I do live through my artist friends. But I don't consider them my servants. And isn't that, after all, the function of art, and of the artist? The artist creates a special world in which he invites others to share so that they can embrace his vision of life. *N'est-ce pas?* Thus art, for the viewer, for the reader, for the concert goer, is nothing if not vicarious participation."

Touché!

My reputation was spreading like wildfire. The patients kept coming. Some of them couldn't pay. I took them on regardless. Pro bono psychiatry. With the Internet at my fingertips, making a diagnosis was a piece of cake. Mary Ann, I decided, was a classic case of penis envy. Belén, obviously the Electra Syndrome. Jeff, my very tall patient, was a neurasthenic. He'd fallen in love with a midget and things hadn't worked out. Following the affair, he became profoundly depressed and couldn't get out of bed in the morning. I prescribed exercise: handball and calisthenics. Probably a horseradish enema would have been a better choice.

Meanwhile, I was hopping down the bunny trail with Belén, the Bump-Bump Girl. But I knew it couldn't go on much longer. Belén was a hell of a nice lady. She was a sweetheart. But the magic wasn't there. I said before that it was the bump-bump business that spoiled everything, but it was more than that. We never talked about anything—except her problems. I felt like a rabbit in a trap.

I think she sensed it that day when I tackled the kitchen sink drain at Ferncrest Manor with my wrenches and whatnot. She sensed, I mean, that I wanted to get away from her. I was at the end of my tether. It wasn't just her, but the clogged-up sink, and the bogus psychotherapy, and the whole stupid, stinking mess that I'd somehow gotten myself into.

Belén sensed that I was going to leave her, and that made her passionate as hell. We got together in the linen closet. She was wearing the white angora sweater that I loved. My angora bunny girl! Her little pink nose was all a-twinkle with excitement. We kissed and kissed.

"I'm all wet for you," she whispered, tugging my zipper down. "I want you inside me."

I pushed her back on top of a stack of folded sheets. The door of the linen closet was half open, but I didn't care. We were hot, so hot. *My angora bunny girl!* I hiked up her skirt, opened her up with my fingers, and we were off to the races.

"*Oof!* Oh God, give it to me! Oh, baby! *Oh! Oh!* Oh, wait a minute, Darling…"

"What? What is it, honey?"

"Remember, no bump-bump!"

But the plumbing nightmare, the sink drain. How did it begin? Let me see. She asked me if I could repair Ferncrest Manor's stopped-up kitchen sink, and I foolishly said yes. Why did I say yes? Inflated ego, I suppose. Clinically significant? Definitely. Masochistic tendencies? You bet!

It went quite well at first. I got the U-shaped sink trap off without any trouble. But then the water from the stopped-up sink flooded the kitchen floor. I'd forgotten to put a bucket under the trap.

Next I attacked the open pipe that led down to the cellar with a rented plumbing snake. I held my breath as I cautiously twisted the handle. Would it work? *Ixnay!* The pipe was packed solid. Then the damn thing "burped," spattering me with the foulest-smelling black gunk I've ever seen. The maid, in her tidy apron, glared at me as if I were something that had crawled out from under the wallpaper.

I was discouraged, but still in no mood to quit. My inflated ego wouldn't allow it. Besides, I had a bright idea. I went down to the cellar, found the pipe, broke the joint above my head with my pipe wrench, and worked the snake upward toward the sink. I seemed to be making headway when—*whoosh*—the whole solid mess in the pipe suddenly spurted out, drenching me with putrid black muck.

When I got back up to the kitchen it turns out that the Ferncrest owner, or district manager, had stopped by. A real pruneface with the frizzy orange hair of a lady orangutan. I stood there, speechless, covered with sludge, a pipe wrench dangling from my paw.

"I'd like to have a word with your plumber, if you don't mind, Belén."

"He's not my plumber. He's my psychiatrist."

Sometimes it's best to just walk away from problems, rather than try to solve them. After Pruneface left, Belén and I sat at the kitchen table and had a whiskey, then another. I was getting pretty sozzled and I was feeling so damned desperate that I wanted to confess to Belén, confess everything, get it all off my chest.

"I'm not a plumber and I'm not a psychiatrist and I'm not an anarchist and I'm not in love with you!"

I came within an inch of saying it, but characteristically, and true to form, I kept silent, and a golden opportunity flitted away.

I know I should have been able to balance everything, but somehow I couldn't do it. I was making money, yes, but everything seemed to be coming apart. It was an uneasy period for me. Several times I felt like the best thing to do was just cut and run, leave town, start over again somewhere else.

13

I DID MANAGE TO GET AWAY from Belén for a few days when Juan Tomás's ex-brother-in-law, Lance Bondurant, blew into town from Amsterdam. Lance was, in Juan Tomás's words, 'scandalously rich, shockingly handsome and swinishly decadent,' and he was looking for a drinking buddy to accompany him on a trip to Palm Springs. Juan Tomás, quite naturally, suggested me.

"You know, it's strange to relate," Juan Tomás said as we had a drink in the office, "but Lance Bondurant, the Playboy of the Western World, is a very lonely man. I'd go myself, but I really can't now, not with Nittaya. You understand, I'm sure, Old Sport."

"Yes, perfectly, JT."

"Nittaya calls me nearly every day. She's a wonderful girl, one in a million. Her parents' village is somewhere in Nong Bua Lamphu in the far North of Thailand. They're rice farmers, desperately poor. Their roof blew off, so I sent them some money and it's back on now. Nittaya's father was worried that I might sell her. As a sex slave, I mean, to the Americans. Can you imagine? I had a Thai friend in Alicante vouch for me. I'll be sending a dowry of one thousand pounds when the time comes. It's a marriage…a marriage made in heaven."

"I'm happy for you."

"But about Lance… Lance and I have remained friends all these years. Can you believe that? It's funny. With some of my marriages, it worked out that way. I remained friends with the in-laws, and sometimes even with the wives. With others, I made a complete break. But Lance… Every so often he'd sweep into town and whisk me off for an adventure. Tits and champagne, you know. This was back in the old days, I mean. Ah, Jerzy, I'll never forget those promenades on the deck of the Sagafjord. Of course Lance got all the girls, and I had to be content with the scrapings. Well, it's probably better than I would have done on my own! Last time I saw Lance we sailed from New York to Southampton on the QE2. We hopped over to Munich just in time for Oktoberfest, went to a party in Schwabig near the Englischer Garten and I ended up getting the crabs from a barefoot contessa from Woodland Hills."

Juan Tomás showed me a twenty year old photo of a deeply tanned Lance in an Armani three-button blazer with windblown hair and a million-dollar grin.

"Oh, he's older now, a little heavy in the jowls, I imagine, but I'd be willing to bet that the old magic is still there, the old Lance Bondurant floy-floy. Of course he does have his quirks, like any confirmed bachelor, and I'm not saying he doesn't. Well, you'll find out."

The next day I packed a change of clothes and my toothbrush and Lance picked me up in a sleek Lincoln town car. He was wearing the same Armani three-button blazer he'd sported in the photo from the slim and elegant days when he and Juan Tomás sailed to French Polynesia on the Tahitian Princess, only now he was busting out of it like a sausage. Still, it was there, the magic, I mean, the floy-floy, as Juan Tomás had predicted, and yet…I don't know quite how to put it. Despite his robust health and his glowing tan, there was something faintly moribund about Lance Bondurant. I couldn't help thinking of him as a patient for whom the whole world is nothing but a jolly and well-appointed sanitarium. Lance was a sun king anesthetized by the brilliance of his own halo. It was as if he he'd permitted himself to be embalmed in money.

"That fettuccine alfredo I ate last night on the plane is lying there inside me like a brick," he said, expertly piloting the Lincoln with two fingers on the wheel. "I've got a good one coming on. Could even be a bowl-ringer. There's nothing like a good shit, Jerzy. It's better than sex."

Lance's voice had the resonance of polished mahogany. Even sitting behind the wheel with just the two of us in the car Lance seemed to be basking in a perfumed ambiance of bouncing tits and clinking champagne glasses. His skin had a pampered glow, as though he'd spent the night in a sarcophagus packed with expensive cold cream.

A mile or two down the road, Lance pulls a hammered silver flask out of the glove compartment and offers me a swig of Bushmill's. "The best revenge, Jerzy, is living well," he murmurs, his voice dripping with mahogany. And he flashes that sensational grin of his. At the same time his canny brown eyes are watching for my reaction. It's as if he's practicing and he wants to make certain that his charming manner will work on the cuties we're sure to meet later in Palm Springs.

"I used to take this flask to the Cornell games," he says. "That's where I met this Janina girl I was telling Juan Tomás about last night. She was a Polack but she had a nice ass. She sucked me off in the frat house after the game. I gave her the old platinum pearls—right down the throat. After she swallowed my cum, she told me she loved me. I lifted my leg and farted in her face. Later she mailed me her Catholic high school graduation photo. 'All my love, forever, Janina,' she wrote on it. I propped the picture up in the urinal at the fraternity house and all the brothers pissed on it. You get your rocks off and you move on, Jerzy. No chains, no pains."

We arrive in Palm Springs and go directly to the Chart

House for drinks and a delightful dinner. Lance is relaxed. The soft lighting brings out an eerie salmon pinkness that shines through his peachy tan—almost as if his handsome face were an artificial sunset created by the embalmer's needle—as he talks easily about an encounter with a stewardess on the flight from Amsterdam. They locked themselves in the toilet and pulled off a quick one.

"Her tits were kinda small, but it was a long flight and I'd already seen the movie twice."

The waiter brings our Grand Marniers and Lance lights up a cigar. "Relaxation. That's what I want this Palm Springs trip of ours to be. Just the two of us, two men of the world. Good food, good wines, good conversation."

After dinner we drive to the condo he's rented. Heart-shaped pool, Jacuzzi, refrigerator pre-stocked with Dom Perignon. We're both weary so we turn in. Relaxation, that's the key. Wonderful to dive into that big fluffy bed with the dinner and the wine and the Grand Marnier gurgling around in my belly. I sleep like a baby.

The next morning we bask like sea turtles in the pool and drink Dom Perignon and eat beluga on little crackers along with slices of Brie and Camembert. Then Lance relaxes in a deck chair with the morning paper. He applies the adhesive to his hairpiece, and I place it for him.

"Hoo, boy," he mutters suddenly, his lips curling in a frown. "That filet mignon I ate last night feels like an ingot of lead inside me. I've got this tremendous pressure...right...in the lower intestine. It's a solid mass. Could very well be a bowl-ringer. That is, if it ever comes out. Oh, Jesus, I'm really paying the price!"

Lance, handsome and charismatic as he was, Playboy of the Western World, Mister Floy-Floy and all that, did have one rather regrettable downside. Lance was obsessed with his bowel movements. He couldn't stop talking about his trips to the toilet, especially when he'd had a drink or two. My diagnosis? Anal expulsive, of course. An excessively liberal potty-training regime during the formative years. It was as plain as the nose on his face. In adulthood, the anal expulsive type is a person who wants to *share* things with you. Going to the toilet, for them, is a social event.

Lance snatches off his reading glasses and jumps to his feet, clutching his midsection. "It's working around in there, and it's...*impacted*. Lot of gas, too. Feels like a major war going on in my guts. Everything's shifting around, like seismic convulsions. There it goes again! The fucking gas bubbles are rising to the surface. Pow!"

We hotfoot it back inside. He's pacing the floor now, wringing his hands, frantically grabbing at his gut. "God, I feel like I've got a volcano in my belly. There it goes! Mount Etna! It's erupting! More incendiary bombs! God, it's backing up! Reverse osmosis! Holy shit! Goddamn, this is serious! Major gas bubbles, Jerzy! Whoops, here I go. I'm heading for the crapper. You can come in if you want to. I don't want to interrupt our conversation. You can sit on the edge of the bathtub and talk to me. That is, if you don't mind the stink bombs. I really like some of the stuff you've been saying. Pop open another bottle of DP, why don't you and—Oh, Jesus! Here it comes! *Oof!* Oh, God! Jerzy? Are you still there? It was a false alarm. Just the same, I feel relieved. I let a pretty good fart. Spattered the bowl a little. Come on in and take a look. Bring your drink.

"You know, just an off-the-wall thought. I've always envied rabbits. You know those perfect little round turds? *Putt-putt-putt!* So easy, you know? And so neat! Wish I could do that. *Putt-putt-putt!* But with me, it's the goddamn waiting period, which goes on forever, and then you deal with the seepage and the backwash and all that, and then you get to the toilet and you get these damned little hard knots. *Plop-plop-plop!* Or else you sit down and—*whoosh-pffttt-ahh!* You know, the liquid stuff. You never get a damn bowl-ringer, or at least only once in a blue moon. How do *you* shit, anyway? *Plop-plop-plop?* Or you do you go *putt-putt-putt*, like a bunny rabbit? Or is it *whoosh-pffttt-ahh?*"

After Lance flushes the toilet I hand him my bottle of

bubbly. I'm sitting on the edge of the bathtub and Lance is sitting on the throne. He takes a long pull of DP and hands the bottle back to me.

"You know, Jerzy, I admire you," he says. "I really do. You're a therapist. You have a direction in life, a purpose, and you're making a contribution to society. I can't tell you how much I admire that, and, if I'm going to be honest, how much I envy you, your position in the world, I mean. Sure, I have my trips, my resorts, my women. But none of it means anything. It's not boredom that's destroying me, it's this emptiness, my own emptiness. It's my superficiality that I despise so much, and yet that's exactly what everyone falls in love with. It's as if I'm nothing but an empty shell.

"When I was a kid at Easter time we used to take eggs and poke holes in the ends with a needle. And then we'd blow all the insides out into a glass. Did you ever do that? And then we'd paint the eggs—the hollow eggs—with all kinds of Easter colors. Well, that's the way I feel. Hollow. A beautiful painted shell. And yet, what I've just said isn't quite true either. It's not a good simile. Is that the word? It's more like a hard-boiled egg. I'm impacted. That's what it is. Whatever was in me that was worth anything has curled up and died. And I can't get it out. Because I'm not empty. I know that. There's something inside me that wants to come out. And maybe that something isn't dead after all, you see. Maybe there's still a spark of life there. But it's buried. It's buried. I can't get in touch with it. In a way, I'm constipated, mentally constipated, spiritually constipated. Maybe I'm just full of shit, who knows?"

14

I GOT BACK TO BEVERLY HILLS just in time to say goodbye to Juan Tomás. He'd closed the *La Vóo de l'Popolo* office and was on his way to the Land of Smiles to marry the beautiful Thai princess, Nittaya. As we were shaking hands he informed me that Belén had found a new love: Edgar. She'd met Edgar at Ferncrest Manor, in fact. I knew I'd miss Belén, but it was probably just as well. She'd undoubtedly realized that I wasn't serious about life. And Edgar was the perfect father figure for her. Edgar was eighty-seven or eighty-eight.

All's well that ends well!

And Jeff had recovered completely from his disastrous affair with the midget, I learned. He was dating a female basketball player. Damian was dating a male basketball player. Phil was dating the midget. This meant that Phil was out of denial at last. No more agonizing over his small stature. And no more bungee jumping. Acceptance. Wisdom. That's my Phil! What a guy.

It had been a golden period. Belén, the great meals, the dinners with Juan Tomás, and finally the trip to Palm Springs with Lance Bondurant. A golden period, yes, but the street came looking for me. I'd gotten used to living high on the hog. I'd lost my edge. Don't imagine for a minute that I didn't think of hitting Juan Tomás up for a loan, but I valued his friendship (as I do today) and I simply couldn't consider it. And now things were back the way they used to be. I was living on Salvation Army Street, corner of Blood Bank Avenue, next door to the Day-Old Bread Store. All around me the current of life was flowing swiftly, but I was becalmed and shipping water, a derelict vessel manned by a skeleton crew. My God, what magnificent desolation! Life in the shadows. *You can look but you can't touch.* It really was magnificent, in a way. I was high on despair. One develops a taste for suffering. Why not admit it?

And so it happened that I met up with Hoffy again. He wasn't broke, he'd been busting suds at a pizza joint, but he was living in his car, the white-trash Trans Am, to save on expenses. He asked me if I wanted to take a little trip— and make some money. I said yes, on both counts.

The next day we went to La Pachanga for the menudo and then we jumped onto the Harbor Freeway and then the San Diego. Soon we were flying past the beach towns: San Juan Capistrano, Dana Point, San Clemente, Oceanside, Carlsbad, Encinitas, Cardiff-by-the-Sea.

Hoffy's idea was that we'd work the Del Mar Fair, which he said was getting ready to open. We'd help set up, then get jobs on the midway, stay for the duration, then get on the tear-down crew. We'd make a bundle, have some fun, and vamoose back to LA.

"Sounds fine to me," I chirped. "Let's bottle up and go."

By the time we got to Del Mar, night had fallen. We parked at the fairgrounds. There were tents, like an Islamic city, mosques and minarets, and a Ferris wheel was spinning silently, ablaze with lights. Loudspeakers brayed in the darkness. The fair was already in progress. We were a few days late. I took this as an omen. I had a sense of impending disaster, as if we were walking into a shitstorm.

I was right, too, as things turned out.

We cruised the midway and had a few beers. And then it happened. Hoffy met up with a dolly from Newport Beach. A perfect little blonde with a hairbrush in her hip pocket. Her name was Serendipity. She wasn't a carny, no, she was a statistician—and her father owned a yacht. The upshot of it was that Hoffy dropped me at Motel 6, paid for the room, pressed a twenty dollar bill into my hand and left me stranded.

Same old Hoffy!

The next morning I was back at the midway. I'd made up my mind that I was going to try for a job, anything, for a few days, in order to get some bucks together. It turned out the only job I could get was in a joint called 'The Monster Mansion', at $8.25 an hour. I took it. The guy hands me a rubber Frankenstein mask, and a black suit, all torn and patched, plus a pair of gigantic shoes with built-up soles at least a foot thick. He gives me a pair of enormous rubber hands.

After I've suited up, he shows me where I'm to station myself. There's a chair, rigged up to look like the electric chair, with coils and transformers and things, and a fake control panel dotted with tiny flashing bulbs. There's a strobe light too, across the room, that's focused on me. We're standing inside a big trailer about the size of a boxcar. The ceiling is painted black. Tiny spokes of light pierce through pinholes in the flimsy plywood walls. There's a raised platform with space for four acts.

The guy went back to his ticket booth. I sat in the electric chair and took off my rubber mask. Through a tear in the black curtain I could see a few people straggling along, gaping at the joint with its flashing lights and lurid billboards. I stared at my rubber Frankenstein face. It was greenish in color, horrendously realistic, with a crimson scar on one cheek and an iron bar that passed through my throat.

The electric chair was comfortable. I was all alone back

there. The other acts hadn't shown up yet. I felt like I was trapped in a holding cell at Abu Ghraib. Just the same, I was enjoying myself. I stared at the flashing strobe. I wasn't trying to get high. I was already high. It's a gorgeous feeling, being in the spotlight. I was sensational! I was somebody: I was Frankenstein. I could feel my ego expanding like a balloon. Yes, I was happy. I was feeling pretty keyed-up. I wanted to get on with the show.

Pretty soon the guy—his name was Nick—came back and told me to put on my mask. I'd been holding it tucked under my arm, like a football helmet. Actually, it was more like a deep-sea diver's helmet, since it completely covered my head and fit tight into the collar of the greasepaint-smeared white shirt Nick had given me along with the moth-eaten undertaker's rig which was miles too big for me and hotter than hell in spite of the moth holes.

I sat in the electric chair sweating like a pig, sucking air through the tiny apertures at the mouth and nose of the rubber mask. I was nearly suffocating. *Whew!* It wasn't so thrilling, once you got down to the nitty-gritty of it. The glamour wears off rather quickly, one finds. The shoes bothered me too, with that foot-thick buildup. When I stood up, I tottered and teetered like an epileptic on ice skates.

The guy clicked a switch and some red and blue lights popped on. He went out to the midway and got some change, then he came back and contemplated me for a moment, puffing on his cigar.

"Listen," he says. "Don't lean against the wall," he says. "There's a weak spot back there that I've got patched up with masking tape. See where I mean, behind you? Okay, got it? *Capish?*"

I could sit in the electric chair if I wanted, he informed me brusquely. "There won't be anything along for thirty minutes or so," he told me as I glared down at him from my towering height. "You might as well cool it until they start coming. You'll know by my voice."

When the people came through I jumped out at them, growling and making goofy noises. That was the job. Some of the people, many of them in fact—and this surprised me—were scared shitless. This was the first of several revelations I was to have during the run of the gig, which lasted fourteen days. But more about that later.

After I'd been at it for about an hour, Nick came back and told me to take a ten-minute breather. I yanked off that stifling rubber helmet and plopped down in the electric chair. The other acts drifted in, blinking their eyes like owls, Dracula, the Mummy and the Wolfman. They'd already suited up. They were holding their helmets in their hands.

The Wolfman had the slot next to me, then Count Dracula, then the Mummy clear down at the other end of the stage. We glanced and nodded at each other, and then Dracula asked me if I had a cigarette. I said, "No, I don't smoke." Then Nick came back again, rubbing his palms together, and said the break was up. He went back to his ticket booth, started the music, and went into his pitch:

"Monsters... *Grrrow!* You'll meet them, on the inside! *Monsters*...from the motion pictures. They are alive. *Monsters... Grrrow!* You'll meet them on the inside and I repeat—they *are* alive!"

Through a hole in the curtain I could see a sector of the midway, the spokes of the Ferris wheel tickling the sky, the organ grinder with his monkey, young girls striding in T-shirts, tits poking your eyes out, kids gnashing cotton candy, even an elephant, marching with mandarin calm and letting go a few smoking balls of dung while snatching at tender grass shoots with his swaying trunk.

The people were coming along now. They began to filter through the joint, sucked in by the spiel and the posters and the music, riding a rail of hope and dizzy yearning, furiously munching popcorn, gnawing at candy apples, swilling beer from paper cups, their faces smeared with mustard and catsup, popeyed, dazzled, dreamy. They were frantic to escape the boredom of their dreary, disappointing lives, if only for a few moments. They wanted nothing less than a prolonged jolt of magic for their three bucks.

The black suit I'm trapped inside of stinks like a rag rescued from the death pits of Treblinka. And the shoes. What a pair of brogans! I didn't have any socks. To take a step hurt like hell. I had to lift my enormous foot high, like a Budweiser Clydesdale, which soon scraped the skin off the tops of my toes. After two hours they were raw and bleeding. My shoes were swimming in blood. I could tell it was blood because it was sticky on the soles of my feet. Burning sweat ran down my legs and trickled into my wounds. Later on I wrapped my tortured feet with some rags, which made the shoes fit better and protected my toes. When I went on a break, I got some ice at a pop stand and dropped it in there. That felt heavenly.

It was strange, inside the joint, with the black crepe paper hanging in tatters from the ceiling, and the canned audio, which simulated growls and sudden jets of steam, and the banks of tiny colored lights constantly blinking on and off. It was Christmassy—almost. "*Whissh... Grrrow!*" It was strange, as I started to say, to look down the line at the other acts. What a gallery of grotesques.

Nearest the door, at the far end, sat the Mummy, wrinkled, bald, with torn ears and filthy burial wrappings dangling like festoons of gangrene. Although he was the most passive of us, somehow the Mummy was by far the most horrific and menacing. He was the image of remorse and vengeance. His rubber features expressed an implacable hatred for the whole human race. There was hate, and also another quality: envy. He envied them, the marks, the parade of humans that filed past us, as the dead must envy the living.

Count Dracula, in the next slot, was sharp-featured, Satanic, a definite Lucifer type. He had arched eyebrows, a little spiked beard, and an unpleasant toothy grin. His molded rubber face reflected an indomitable will and an insatiable cupidity, as though he'd been sharpening his incisors in the dark for at least a thousand years. His eyes were darting flames of lust, his movements lightning quick. He was on the make, eager for blood. Dracula was the most *human* of us. Except for his extraordinary aliveness, he was hardly different from the rank and file. He could have passed in a crowd—*maybe*—on a dark street.

The Wolfman, stationed next to me, was clumsy and bestial, like a satyr. He resembled the great god Pan, but his rubber features were much coarser than the beast-god's. Ferocity was reflected there, and a pathological shyness, and despair, predicated upon the impossibility of ever learning human ways. The lycanthrope was more animal than man, yet human enough to feel the pangs of loneliness. A hopeless oaf, his furry face frozen in a sardonic grin, he was more pathetic than frightening.

What a bestiary. The Mummy, Dracula, the Wolfman and Frankenstein. A quaternity. The Four Horsemen of the Apocalypse, no less.

I, Frankenstein, was the climax. I had top billing. I was the star. I had the extra equipment: the strobe, the electric chair, and the fake lightning bolts. The Mummy had a wooden coffin, propped up behind him like a bass fiddle; the Wolfman had a stack of cinder blocks and a few rusty chains; and Dracula had a canvas backdrop featuring a sketchy, poorly executed painting of a castle. I don't know who the artist was, but it wasn't Piero della Francesca or Pieter Brueghel the Elder, if you know what I mean.

When my break came around, I ventured into the dressing room, which was filthy, smelly, and hardly bigger than a phone booth. There were costumes hanging on hooks. You had to squeeze between them: masks, dangling hands, feathers. King Kong was there, and Tarzan, with his amazing sculptured rubber body, and the Headless Horseman.

I stood in front of the dirty cracked mirror, studying

myself. I had a sickly green face, a livid scar on my left cheek and an iron bar through my neck. The top of my skull was flat, as though I had fallen from a tremendous height and landed on my head. I was a fallen angel, freak, anomaly, botched creation, hyena, monstrosity, geek. I was the monstrous fruit of mistaken hopes and years of insane scientific labors and alchemies. I was the experiment that failed. I was a monster who regards this world with a baleful, uncomprehending eye. I had already died a thousand times, I could see that at a glance, and I had been brought back to life again. I had been resurrected, yes, but in Hell!

All the same, it was great being top banana. I'd sit in the electric chair when the people filed through. I had a little button I could press, under the right armrest. *Bzzzt!* I would electrocute myself. They liked that. I'd leap up, my pants on fire, and clomp around the stage, waving my arms, roaring and hissing. Then I'd march stiffly toward them, arms outstretched, groping blindly, while the banks of lights fizzed and popped around me.

The next morning, at ten, I was back in harness. Things were slow. At two o'clock, Nick came back and told us to take off for a few hours. He was going to close up until evening, he said. As I was getting out of my suit in the tiny dressing room, drenched with sweat, I spotted Count Dracula through a crack in the boards. He was collecting his wages from Nick at the ticket booth. Apparently, he'd had enough.

I stumbled around the midway, wondering what to do with myself. Hungry. No money. I'd squandered my first day's pay on a motel room for the night. I amble toward the lagoon that borders on the fairgrounds. I've decided to soak my feet. My lacerated toes are smarting like crazy.

It's strange to be walking without the gigantic shoes that were heavier than a deep-sea diver's lead boots and made me feel like I had two clubfeet. I feel weightless, breathless, as if my lungs are inflated with helium. I'm defying gravity. The bounce in my stride is fantastic. The hard packed trampoline earth of the midway threatens at every step to fling me skyward like a projectile. Nothing can keep me on the ground. I'm going up, up, like an observation balloon. I'm floating high above the tents and banners. I've reached Heaven's door without really trying.

Now I understand, quite explicitly, why the martyrs wore hair shirts and slept on beds of iron spikes: it feels so good when you stop.

I came to the brink of a blackwater canal that flowed under a railroad trestle, widening on the other side of the bridge into the lagoon itself. The canal is dirty, putrid, but it's flowing. It's oozing like an infected gash. Every now and then a big gob of black snot drifts slowly by, as though a coal miner had cleared out his lungs upstream. They look like membranes, these clots, or plastic bags filled with decayed jellyfish.

I sit down on some soft tufts of grass and slip out of my shoes. I stick my feet in the stinking water. *Bliss.* The canal is a sink, a breeding hole for mosquitoes. I scoop up some of the black water in my cupped hand. It's alive with wigglers, larvae. They're squirming like maggots. All that teeming life. Near the surface of the canal, buff-colored moths with powdery wings are swooping and looping like angels dancing on an onyx mirror.

I sat for a long time on the bank of the canal, gazing down at my wounded feet. "*The Stigmata,*" I whispered, smiling to myself. I repeated the phrase several times. I felt outrageously happy.

Pretty soon a young guy came walking along the bank of the canal. He said hello. I said, "Hello." After he'd been standing there for a while, he asked if he could sit down. I said yes. After another silence, which I wasn't at all anxious to disturb, he pulls a half-pint of Old Cabin Still out of his pocket and asks me politely if I want a drink. Again, I say yes. He takes off his shoes and socks and rolls up his pants and sticks his feet in the water, and we begin talking about one thing and another. The strange thing is, he seems to know me, yet I can't place him for the life of me. It was puzzling, since I rarely forget a face.

Finally I asked him point blank if I hadn't seen him somewhere before. He looked at me in surprise.

"You're Frankenstein, aren't you?" he says. "Yes," I answer. "I'm the Wolfman," he said apologetically.

We shook hands and had a laugh over that. We finished the bottle of Old Cabin Still and he came up with another one. He was just a kid. Chad was his name. He came from Willow Grove, Pennsylvania.

"Do you always work this shift?" he asks me earnestly. I tell him it's only my second day on the job. "Mine, too," he says. He's been sleeping in the stables, he informs me, at the famous Del Mar Track, just a stone's throw from where we're sitting.

Chad and I got to feeling pretty good, and soon it was time to go back to the Monster Mansion. After that we often came back to the same spot at night, on breaks, to sit and get buzzed and soak our feet in the canal. This interlude became a regular part of my routine.

It was beautiful at night at the canal. Peering through skeletons of Ferris wheels and other wreckage of machinery piled high around the canal, I could see the midway, an amazing whirligig of flashing lights, shooting off spores in the darkness like a fantastic mushroom. When the train went through, slam-banging its way across the creaking trestle, my heaven was complete. It was the local, just five cars. A passenger train, Amtrak, out of LA. I saw faces looking out the windows. Commuters. They were pointing, smiling, nudging each other, and laughing. I felt happy for them.

It was better in the evenings, cooler inside the joint, the crowds were better, the people moved faster, and there were girls. Some of them stopped and talked and made dates to meet us later on. Not one of them showed up.

The kid, Chad, and I more or less worked together,

since our acts were right next to each other. At first, except for Chad and myself, the personnel changed almost daily. By the fifth or sixth day a Mexican kid, obviously a wetback, was playing Dracula, and there was an old man, so drunk he could hardly stand, in the Mummy suit. The Mummy didn't have to go through any gyrations, which was lucky for the old man. When the people filed through, he got up and staggered around. It was very convincing. Every so often, when things got slack, the old man would guzzle from a pint of Jack Daniels that he kept hidden in the tattered burial wrappings. The eerie thing was, with the flashing lights and fake lightning bolts and all, the old man's face hardly looked different than the infernal Mummy mask.

I felt sorry for the wetback, Ramon; strange country, no English. He couldn't have been more than fifteen.

Nick, the boss, was a handsome Italian from Marina del Rey. Mr. West Coast Promotion Man. His manner was condescending to say the least. He wore hounds tooth beige slacks, a white shirt, a string tie or sometimes a medallion, and a little Sherlock Holmes hat that perched on his head like a pile of guano.

Nick was a cheap bastard. Eight bucks an hour we got, as I already mentioned. He paid every night, peeling the bills off his oily roll. He took these occasions, as we stood waiting for our money in the stifling trailer, to run us down about our work. Sometimes he mounted the stage and paced up and down, puffing on a cigar while he harangued us. We indulged him. It was just something Nick had to get out of his system. We were all half sloshed anyway, and the Mummy was dead drunk. We drank openly, passing pints of muscatel and cheap whiskey as our master, Boss Tweed, the little lion tamer, paced the floor and laid down the law. We had no hustle, he claimed, and we were too hard on the equipment.

"You take the damn cheap rubber they're making the shit out of nowadays. You know what I mean? You get one little tear started, and *zingo*—there's your investment, shot in the ass! Maybe you fellas think I'm an S.O.B. *Okay!* Okay, do you have any idea what it costs me to keep this joint open? Well? *For one day, I mean!* Take a guess! No hype, fellas. I don't bullshit anybody, you know that!"

He even threatened to take something out of Chad's pay, because, he claimed, Chad had chewed holes in the rubber Wolfman mask. The kid had reason to chew. He was nervous, he was broke, he was running from the law, and he had a dose of the clap. I urged him to see a doctor, but he wouldn't listen to me. Like the *mojado*, Ramon, he was afraid of being seen. *Life in the shadows!*

It pissed me off, the way Nick rode the Mexican kid and the old man. The weaker you were, the quicker he was to pounce on you. That was the way Nick saw it.

I'm thinking of one night when things were slow. On a break, we were steaming in our wet clothes, holding our helmets in our laps like gladiators. The Mummy was eating a ham sandwich, chewing wearily, smacking his toothless gums like an ancient turtle, and washing the sandwich down with gulps from his pint of Jack Daniels. Nick comes back, puffing his cigar, brisk and chipper in a fresh shirt.

"You fellas get your masks on now," he says. "And, Mummy, a little more life out of you. *Capish?* If you can't step and fetch, I'll get myself another boy! You freaks better listen up. I don't shuck and jive! You better remember one thing, gentlemen: *Don't fuck with Hoppy!*

"Frankenstein," he adds, with a threatening glance at me, "stay behind the curtain. At all times. *Capish?*"

He said this to me because earlier that night I'd been standing on the edge of the platform behind the ticket booth, peering through the torn black curtain like the Phantom of the Opera. I was ogling the crowd, and they loved it. It was good theater, by God! But Mr. Big didn't like being upstaged. He was jealous, that was the long and short of it. When, later on that same night, he came back and suggested casually to me that I'd been spending too much time sitting in the electric chair, I told him flatly to kiss my ass. After that, he never hassled me. But that night, as I say, he rode the Mexican kid and the old man to death.

I felt sorry for the old man. In spite of the stayin' and keepin' power of Jack Daniels, or maybe because of it, he was coming apart at the seams. Afternoons, getting into his Mummy rig, he quaked and shivered like a dog shitting peach seeds. Clearly, the old fossil was on his last legs.

ONE NIGHT Nick had a brainstorm. He wanted me to change positions with the Mummy—and he offered to up my pay fifty cents an hour. I said nothing doing. For one thing, I knew the old man could never navigate in those lead boots. It would have killed him to play Frankenstein. Maybe that was just what Nick wanted— revenge. He didn't like the old man. And he wanted to belittle me, because I was a thorn in his side.

But that wasn't the reason I wouldn't make the switch. It wasn't as noble as all that. I wasn't looking out for the old man, I was looking out for myself. Whenever the old man ripped off his Mummy mask and pulled at his pint of Jack Daniels, I studied his face. A yellow ribbon of snot flowed like a river from his right nostril. He sucked the mucous into his toothless mouth. His lips were cracked and bleeding, and when he put on the mask you could see his lips bleeding through the Mummy's rubber mouth. So I imagined the inside of the Mummy mask coated with snot and the froth of his whiskey spit and the blood from his cracked lips. I thought of myself putting on the old man's ungodly rig, and I realized that I simply couldn't do it. Not for $8.75 an hour. Not for any price.

The days wore on. Chad, the Wolfman, stuck to me like a shadow. I got used to it, his shaggy animal presence always at my side. The kid was used up. He wanted me to tell him what to do. I advised him to go to a rescue mission in San Diego, or to the Salvation Army, and turn himself in. Even to the cops.

"First offense," I warbled, "...reduced to a misdemeanor..."

I didn't know what Chad's crime was, but I judged from his character that it wasn't anything much. Maybe he ripped somebody off for a fifty-dollar watch, or he stole a car and smashed it up, or knocked up somebody's daughter. It was something trivial. I tried to paint a rosy picture of a stay in the prison hospital, three hots and a cot, the delectable nurses, the drugs, but he wasn't buying it. I couldn't blame him. I wouldn't have gone either.

I made runs to the liquor store for the old man. He was too drunk to walk. The Mexican kid and Chad confronted me solemnly, like obedient children. They were all clinging to me. I had nothing to offer them. They were drowning men, sinking into quicksand. They were grabbing at straws. For some reason, I looked like a lifeboat to them, but I was breaking my balls trying to keep *myself* afloat. Couldn't they see that?

One afternoon it rained. What a blessing. Huge scattered drops fizzed on the dusty ground. The midway became a sea of slick mud swimming with peanut shells and cigarette butts and crumpled cones of cotton candy that had been trampled underfoot. Everything was melting.

I stood under the awning of a hamburger stand drinking beer from a paper cup. I watched the organ grinder vigorously scrub his bedraggled monkey with a bath towel. The monkey sneezed. The guy looked worried.

I sat under the railroad trestle with a pint of tokay. The canal was overflowing its banks. I gazed back at the midway. In the rain, the carnival looked like a city sinking beneath the waves.

By now my stigmata had developed calluses. I no longer needed ice inside the boots. I bought it anyway, a bag each night. *Luxury.* I also bought a thick pair of socks. I had the job down pat. But I was beginning to worry about the ice in my shoes, about my wet feet. Sitting in the electric chair, maybe I would get sizzled, with those sopping feet and all. This had never happened before—the worry, the apprehension, I mean. For every plus there's a minus, one discovers.

All in all, it was fourteen days of torture, frequently ten or twelve hours a day. What a steam bath! I lost ten pounds. Some nights I drank whiskey with Chad, but mostly I drank muscatel from a pint that I kept under my habit. The muscatel helped a little, but the truth is, my heart wasn't in it—in getting looped, I mean. I was simply beating a dead horse. The truth is, as it turns out, you can't stay high in Hell. If you could, it wouldn't be Hell. No matter how high you get, you're still below sea level. All you can hope to do is alleviate the pain of existence.

Then came the night the old man passed out. It was near the end of my Season in Hell. There were just two days to go. The old man was reeling around, as usual, growling at the people, when suddenly he collapsed. Dracula quickly stepped over to help him up. The old man stood there, swaying. He wobbled for a moment, and then he tore off the Mummy mask and threw up. Then he fell backwards, smashing into his flimsy coffin. He knocked it helter-skelter, splintering the bender boards. He hit the deck and lay there like a sack of cement. The marks loved it; they thought it was part of the script.

Right away Nick comes back, mumbling under his breath, and orders Dracula and me to carry the Mummy out and lay him out on the ground behind the joint. He orders us to strip off the burial wrappings, and then he brings the old man around with a shot of water in the face and gives him his walking papers.

"Good riddance," he said, dusting off his hands. "I'll be damned if I'm going to have that old bastard puking inside the joint. The place already stinks like a shithouse. This is the last time I'm hiring a lush!"

Almost as an afterthought, he peeled some bills off his

roll and tossed them on the old man's chest. I stood up quickly. I was furious. Somehow this contemptuous gesture was the last straw. I wanted to flatten Nick, but I knew it would mean jail for me. I didn't have an address. I didn't even have a driver's license. Nick held his ground. *Don't fuck with Hoppy!* He stared at me insolently. He knew damn well I wasn't going to hit him. After he marched off, I knelt down and stuffed the bills into the old man's pocket.

The old man barfs again. I hold his head. I burp him like a baby to keep him from drowning in his whiskey vomit. I hoist him to his feet. I want to see if he can navigate. He can't. He collapses. He doesn't have long to go. I sense that. This Mummy act at the Del Mar Fair is the old man's swan song.

I peer into his face. I stare at the powdery wrinkles under his eyes. It's the powder from the inside of the mask. The eyes themselves are blank, black and festering like the canal. The mind flowing behind them has already returned to the source, to the fertility of chaos.

I give the old man some water. He spits it out. He sputters and gags. He acts like I tried to poison him. Then I give him a shot of muscatel. He glugs it down. I feed him like a baby, cradling him in my arms. I'm still in costume, still wearing my Frankenstein mask. Finally, I give him the bottle, and he crawls off into some tall weeds. I cover him with newspapers.

The Mexican kid, the *jovencito*, Ramon, quit that same night. I never saw him again. Chad switched to being Count Dracula, and Nick hired another *mojado* to fill the Wolfman slot for the final two days. He dropped the Mummy act altogether. He hung the bedraggled rubber suit on a hook in the dressing room, and afterwards, when I saw it hanging there like an empty cocoon, I thought of the old man.

ALL IN ALL, it was some gig. But the reactions of the

people that passed through the joint were the most curious part about it. Many of them, incredible as it sounds, were scared out of their wits. Some actually burst into tears. Others flew into a rage. They cursed and spat. They reviled me. It was uncanny. I never knew what to expect. I even had a jamoke pull a knife on me. I got hit with a basket of rotten tomatoes. Some society bitch tried to stick me with a hatpin. She came right up on stage after me. She was crazed with hatred. They hated me. And they were right in heaping me with abuse, right in venting their indignation, because they'd paid their three bucks.

I was the scapegoat, the Jew, the exile, the nemesis, the pariah. I was Frankenstein, Moloch, Goliath, Minotaur. I was the grinning hyena that waits at the end of the night. I was The Reason: fucking car won't start, baby's crying, bastards are after you for back payments. Arthritis, termites, dandruff, haven't had a decent orgasm in five years, wrinkles, dirty dishes, bills piling up, muggy weather, ants, lawnmower's broken, toilet clogged, phone jangling. All the little Golgothas. *Jesus, it hasn't been any fairytale!*

This was the voice of the herd, their howling chorus, and their common complaint. They saw me and said, '*here's the scum who's responsible!*' They needed someone to hate, a tangible focus for their remorse and disappointment, and I'd been elected, the projection of their own inner hell. I was everything that had been swept under the rug, denied, revoked, exiled. They came, knowingly or not, to confront the dark side of their nature, and I was it. They came to embrace, with arms and legs in the primitive darkness, everything they had banished from their tidy little lives. My crucifixion was an exercise in exoneration and detachment.

I went through my gyrations mechanically. I sat in the electric chair and endured their imprecations, but inwardly I was calm and serene. *I* was intact. It was they who were on display.

I came to feel, toward the end of my Season in Hell, that I had occupied a unique and privileged position, that I had been able to dispense a valuable service. Strangers filed into my dominion, I confronted them and they confronted me. In darkness, bare wires touched, sparks flew, and the circuit was completed. I had been, for a time, a conduit through which a vital, renewing current flowed.

15

TODAY WAS A BONANZA DAY. Fourteen hours without a break. I made five batches of everything: twenty-five hundred donuts. A forest of mouths at the counter snapped them up. I got off at four in the afternoon. Bottomly simply called a halt. When I hung up my apron, there wasn't a donut left in the place. What an extravaganza!

It's a pleasure when everything's right. I pound the dough, I push it around, I slam it down on the board; I roll it out. A squirt of the squeeze bottle, fold it over—*slam!* Stamp it with the cutter, a twist of the wrist, I toss the rings in the air and twirl them on my thumb to size. This is the trick of getting them round. It's centrifugal force. I slide them, nice and easy, perfect zeroes, onto the rack, twenty-five rings per rack. Into the proof box: twenty minutes, then I sink the rack and float the puffed-up rings in the hot grease. It's not so bad, once the people start coming in and somebody plays the jukebox. There's always a little gallery at the counter, and then of course there's Lisa the waitress to play grab-ass with. Lisa is very young, very cute. She calls me 'Donny Donut'.

Yesterday I was filling the jelly donuts under

Bottomly's watchful eye. I crank the handle. *Sploop!* I shoot them full of jelly, exactly one pull and a half, the way he showed me. Bottomly's watching me like a hawk. He's counting every squirt. He's muttering under his breath, calculating, adding it all up.

Bottomly's first name is Duncan. He spells it 'Dunken', because of the donuts. Dunken Donuts is the only non-Cambodian donut shop in Los Angeles. Bottomly is not only white, he's the very quintessence of whiteness. With his forearms and apron covered in white flour, he looks exactly like an unbaked biscuit.

I begin work each day at 2:00 a.m. Around four-thirty, Nat arrives in an old car that nearly collapses at the curbside. Mustache, muscles, tattoos. A worn face. He reads the newspaper while he demolishes two buttermilk donuts and eight or ten cups of coffee. Painstakingly, he folds the newspaper lengthwise in columns. He pores over that newspaper as if he were deciphering the Mayan Codex. Every day it's the same; after his second buttermilk donut, he gets up and plays 'San Antonio Rose' on the jukebox.

The other morning Mrs. Bottomly was standing on a chair unscrewing a light bulb. Newspaper Nat reaches over the counter and tries to pinch her ass. She puts the freeze on him, pronto. Mrs. Bottomly is an icicle. Not a drop of fun in this lady.

"Nat," she says evenly, keeping her eyes on her work, "I'll tell you once more: Either you act like a gentleman or you can get out."

"Aw, come on, Edwina..."

"Nat, I mean it now."

I talk about Bottomly watching the portions, but actually it's Edwina. She's the one measuring and counting, not Bottomly. He's just a pimple on her ass. He's a factotum, a biscuit boy. He's a squidge. That's what I call him, in fact, 'the Squidge'. Edwina is the power behind the throne.

For example, she tells me not to bring the screen down on the cinnamon rolls, which is the way Bottomly taught me to do it, because it makes better cinnamon rolls. Behind the counter she showed me the *new* way, her way. I wasn't impressed. She was going for volume, not quality. She wants the rolls to appear big, even if they're not. Edwina's cinnamon rolls are bloated and shapeless. I like to bring the screen down on them, keep them crisp, flat, uniform. A cinnamon roll is not an observation balloon. It's not a gasbag full of hot air. I simply won't do it Edwina's way. I can't.

The other morning I came to work at 2:00 a.m. as usual and the glass door was smashed. The cops were already there. They questioned me. Did I see anybody? *Nobody. I just got here.* I unlock the shattered door and switch on the lights. I punch my card. I start the coffee machine. I begin mixing the first batch. Crazy Jaime, always my first customer, is standing outside near the cop car. He's wearing an Eighth Army overcoat, mismatched socks, no shoes. The cop follows me around with a clipboard. Anything taken? *Nothing.* Clearly it's a case of vandalism.

Everybody knows Crazy Jaime. He spends his days wandering. You see him talking to kids all over the barrio. He's a hero on the streets. Everybody likes Crazy Jaime, even Mrs. Bottomly. She reserves her tenderness for the maimed.

Crazy Jaime is my companion on long nights as I roll out the dough. The first thing he does after sitting down at the counter is empty out his pockets. He puts everything on the counter, exactly as if he were being booked at the police station. He buys a bag of day old donuts for a dollar. I bring him a cup of coffee. The coffee is on the house. That's understood from the start.

After Crazy Jaime has eaten his way through his bag of stale donuts, he decides to brush his teeth. He picks up his toothbrush off the counter and asks me for a glass of water. He sprinkles salt on the toothbrush, takes a mouthful of water, scrubs away for a while, and spits in the glass. Next he calls for the restroom key. He has to take a shit. He treats me like an attendant.

When Crazy Jaime returns from the toilet, he starts in on the reading. Crazy Jaime stuffs his pockets with leaflets, travel brochures, pages torn from magazines and scraps of newspaper he picks up on his meanderings. These he reads aloud to me, sitting at the counter, serious as a judge. It goes on for hours. He reads English very well, with hardly a trace of an accent.

Crazy Jaime is a man of many voices. When he tells me in Spanish about how his mother fried tortillas in grease and sugared them to make *buñelos*, his voice is soft and nostalgic, musical. When he talks about his adult life, his language becomes harsh and slangy, the Spanish of the barrio. And when he reads in English, it's crisp and officious, like a radio announcer.

"Three days, two nights...deluxe room...unlimited golf...tennis...bicycle built for two...Mai Tais in the famous Barefoot Bar..."

On and on, like a river. I hate to bother him—after all, he *is* insane—but he's driving me crazy. While I'm cutting out the tarts, I turn on the radio: some idiot disc jockey, worse than Jaime. I switch off the radio.

"Eternal Hills Memorial Park...mortuary, mausoleum, crematory, all in one convenient location..."

Dickie the Wonder Bread Man comes in right after Newspaper Nat, clamping an unlit cigar in his bulldog jaw. He's a pint-sized guy, a perfect little beer keg. Always the same brilliant smile, but mechanical, like a wind-up toy. He reads a paperback novel while he munches his fodder, one glazed and two cups of coffee.

At 5:15, it's the two Acme janitors, the flower truck driver and Handsome Tony with his lunch pail. Handsome Tony: two glazed, one cinnamon twist, three cups of coffee. He reads the sports page. Handsome Tony was once a high school hero. Now he's serving time in the factory. He's balding but hard as a rock. Handsome Tony's face might have been stamped on a Roman coin. It's the face of a general, a gladiator, an emperor. Tony was destined for great things. Maybe not the Forum Romanum, but Yankee Stadium at the very least.

"How's it going, Tony?"

"One day is like another," he says bitterly, his powerful jaws working as he mangles a glazed donut. Handsome Tony is the hero of a drama that was never written, never produced.

Crazy Jaime, Newspaper Nat, Handsome Tony and Dickie the Wonder Bread Man. Then there's Bea, Beatrice, Beatriz del Lago, the knit shop lady. She orders a cake donut with chocolate sprinkles and dunks it in her coffee. Beatriz del Lago keeps cats, and they say she was once a Hollywood costume designer. I call Beatriz del Lago 'the Lady of Shalott' because she weaves enormous skeins of words about Hollywood's Golden Era, a vintage tapestry invested with mythos and crawling with cat dander.

On Sundays a silver Rolls Royce pulls up out front and a man gets out with a two hundred-pound dog on a leash. The man is dressed for jogging. He comes in around four-thirty and orders a dozen glazed and three cinnamon rolls, then feeds it all to the dog. Somehow it pisses me off to see that big slobbery brute gulping down my creations, especially the cinnamon rolls. But I tell myself, that's ridiculous, I just work here.

Actually, the donut is a perfect art form. The glazed donuts, round, tight, shining; the buttermilks, crisp, broken open, smoking hot… Beautiful! Art should be devoured. No museums.

One day last week things were slow. Lisa was on duty. At the counter, it was just Crazy Jaime and the Lady of Shalott. And Newspaper Nat. Newspaper Nat had just punched 'San Antonio Rose' on the jukebox. The Squidge wasn't around, and the Red Queen was in the counting house, counting out the money; so Lisa and I ventured into the pantry. I got down on my knees next to an open bag of pastry flour and jerked Lisa's panties down.

"Donny Donut? What are you doing, Donny Donut? Oh! Oh, my God!"

"Want me to stop?"

"No! Yes! No! Don't! I mean, don't stop! Oh, Donny…"

The flour is crawling with weevils, I notice, shiny black poppy seeds that move and squirm and hop. And all around me, sweetness: I'm dipping my tongue into a living cinnamon roll.

"*Oh! Oh! Oh! Ohh…*"

I get to my feet. Lisa pulls up her panties and kisses me again and again, her eyes brimming with tears.

"Oh, Baby, Baby. That's my Donny. That's my Donny Donut!"

A FEW WEEKS LATER, a savage earthquake has put me on edge. I seem to be standing on the deck of a rolling, pitching ship. Apparently this city, and the very terrain on which it perches, are nothing more than the crust of a baked apple. Within the apple, a molten flux, shifting grids, bubbling magma: everything is slipping and sliding…

A stroll along Wilshire. The slender, beautifully manicured palm trees sway in the breeze. The smog tastes like machine oil. The jacaranda trees are in full bloom and the sidewalks are strewn with papery lavender bells. Some Japanese girls are standing outside the Wilshire Royale Hotel, clutching their cameras, their lips glistening like crushed raspberries. As I pass by, I inhale their fragrance.

Alexandria Street. The ragged flapping of pigeons' wings, a man tap-tapping with his blind-stick, the shrieks of seagulls as they pillage a dumpster. I catch the #21 heading downtown.

Orange flames erupt from the LA Prime Matter sculpture, Wilshire and Figeroa. Arco Plaza, the musical gurgle of water and the laughter of children playing and climbing, mesmerized by the glittering coins in the fountain.

The thing with Lisa is heating up. She had a brief fling with another guy, a soldier, but he shipped out to the slaughterhouse in Iraq. I'm still her Donny Donut, she says.

I like my job at Dunken Donuts, but there's a downside. It's called paranoia. Rampart Precinct has the highest crime rate in the city. Sometimes at night when I'm rolling out the dough I can hear the chatter of automatic weapons fire. We're right in the middle of Little Central America here. And this place is a goldfish bowl.

Two nights ago, for example. Here I am flipping the donuts. It's just Crazy Jaime and me. Three cholos cruise by in a low-rider. They're probably looking to jack the place. I'm feeling very vulnerable and very *white*. The cholos cruise by again. My mouth is dry; my pulse is racing. Do they know there's next to nothing in the cash register? And if I tell them, will they believe me? I'm a sitting duck. I'm just a donut frying in fat.

I never thought I'd be happy to see the Squidge with that dough-ball fetus-face of his, but when he walked into the shop I began to breathe a little easier. Then Newspaper Nat came in and the Squidge left, and the rest of the crew happened along too: Dickie the Wonder Bread Man, Handsome Tony, and the others. I mixed another batch... I cut out perfect zeroes, twirl them on my thumb, pop them in the proofer, float them in the fat, flip them with the sticks, and I'm feeling mellow once again.

I'm feeling so relieved that I'm even beginning to enjoy the Lady of Shalott's unending tapestry of words.

"*You should be kissed, Scarlett, and often, and by someone who knows how...*"

Meanwhile, Crazy Jaime is running on like an idiot savant. "*There will be a potluck dinner Sunday night at the Jewish Community Center...*"

The gang's all here! I'm flipping the donuts, and Jaime

is babbling. Newspaper Nat finishes his second buttermilk donut and plays 'San Antonio Rose' on the jukebox. Dickie the Wonder Bread Man looks up from his paperback novel and flashes that brilliant mechanical smile of his, his tiny teeth wobbling like wooden pegs.

Handsome Tony smiles bitterly as he stirs his java. Where did he go wrong? How did Joe DiMaggio wind up in this dismal end-of-the-world donut shop with a crazy Mexican, a failed writer, a loony old lady and Dickie the Wonder Bread Man?

But I was happy. I was even happy when the silver Rolls Royce puke walked in with his great slavering dog. And in a few minutes, I tell myself as I lift my latest batch off the glazing screen, Lisa will be here and it'll be Donny Donut time once again.

But the very next night was the night the Indians came in. Two of them. The tall one was wearing a black hat with silver conchos and a shiny black leather vest over his bare torso. His long brown arms were covered with jail tattoos, Pachuco marks and maybe needle tracks. He was the Exterminating Angel personified. I tried being cordial in English and Spanish. No response. Just those hard black eyes glittering under the hat brim.

That silence was more devastating than any accusation they might have hurled at me. *They don't speak my language*, I'm thinking. Or else they speak Arapaho or Blackfoot or Flathead Salish. Or Potawatomie or Powhatan, or Pueblo, or maybe Shawnee or Shoshone. Or Havasupai or Haudenosaunee, or Oneida, Onondaga, Lakota, Montauk or Tuscarora or Wolastoqiyik. Maybe their language is vengeance. I realize that it's altogether fitting and proper, but I don't want to be the sacrificial lamb. I think of telling them that the register is closed, but I didn't want to say the word 'register'. I quickly put a dozen glazed donuts in a box and pour two takeout cups of coffee.

"It's on the house, gentlemen."

Crazy Jaime, at the counter, hardly looks up from his

reading.

"The Cub Scout mothers of Laguna Nigel will sponsor a pancake breakfast at the Methodist Church…"

Paranoia creates its own world: silent, deadly, logical, and graceful as a ballet. It's all maya, illusion. When the assassins finally galloped off into the desert, I realized that they might very well have been just a couple of guys on their way to work.

All the same, Lisa or no Lisa, I think my Donut Days are coming to a close.

16

I WAS SITTING at an alfresco table at Hollywood Passage, the bricked arcade of the International Restaurant, a homey little place on Hollywood Boulevard across the street from the Wax Museum. I'd just come from La Pachanga and was pleasantly blotto. And who shows up but Danira, in a faux chinchilla jacket and a black sombrero. How long had it been? Months and months.

"It's good to see you," she murmured, and she kissed me hard, on the mouth. I realized that she was smashed too. Danira was ripped to the tits, and she was terribly distraught.

It turned out that her troubles revolved around Juan Tomás, her old flame. Just weeks after marrying Nittaya in Bangkok, and getting her settled at his villa in Alicante, he'd flown back to LA alone to wrap up a few loose ends, and Danira was one of them. They'd moved into a beach house in Santa Monica and everything was ducky, but now they'd broken up and he'd gone back to Alicante.

I tried to comfort her, but she couldn't stop crying. Juan Tomás was more than an old flame, I learned. He'd been Danira's first love, or her first real love. They'd spent a summer together in Lawrence Durrell's villa on the island of Corfu when she was twenty-one. Half of the United States Navy had marched between Danira's legs since then, but that onslaught had done nothing to erase the memory of that summer of love on Corfu with the charming Englishman. And here she was, Danira, in my arms, bawling like a baby.

Somehow her tears—her vulnerability—excited me. Normally, Danira was courageous, optimistic, completely in charge. It was Danira who in the past had dictated the terms of our relationship. She was the strong one and I was the supplicant, a pickle floating in brine, a halibut begging to be speared. Now it was my turn. Danira was wounded, weakened—helpless, almost—in my hands. I have to admit that I was terribly turned on.

"Come on, let's go," I said, grabbing her roughly by the shoulders. "I'm taking you home."

We left the restaurant and walked along Hollywood Boulevard, looking for a taxi. It was just a few days before Halloween and in every storefront there were ghoulish displays and flashing lights, and somehow it all seemed perfect because it's always Halloween on Hollywood Boulevard.

Finally, I hailed a taxi, and inside the taxi I shoved Danira to the floor, between my knees, and placed her hand on my bursting fly.

Danira didn't wait for an engraved invitation. She jerked my pants down and sucked frantically, as if only my orgasm could assuage her sorrow. I could feel her cool wet tears on my thighs as she bobbed her head up and down. After a moment or two, I was ready to squirt. She pulled her mouth off me and gazed up at me adoringly.

"Do you want me to keep doing it?" she whispered in that maddening little girl voice of hers.

A moment later, I went off like a fire hose, spewing my jellied essence all over her face.

"Did you like that, Baby?" she whispered. "I'm all wet

for you, do you realize that? I want you to toy-fuck me. I want you to hurt me. Will you do it?"

We got out of the taxi at the beach house near the Santa Monica pier. Danira paid. I don't know how much the fare was, but it must have been a war debt. The sky was crawling with stars. It was a balmy night and you could smell the kelp rotting on the beach. We sat at the kitchen table and drank a bottle of white zinfandel. Danira went on and on about Juan Tomás. I tried to calm her down, but it was useless, she was out of control.

After a few moments of desperate sobbing, she jumped up from the table and brought a sheaf of poems scrawled on white typewriter paper with a felt-tip pen. Juan Tomás had written her a poem every day, she informed me proudly, which struck me as strange because Juan Tomás had repeatedly told me that he didn't have a creative bone in his body.

I read the first poem aloud: *"Plena mujer, manzana carnal, luna caliente…"*

Immediately, I recognized those lines. *Pablo Neruda!* What a bastard he was, passing off Pablo Neruda's poetry as his own on poor, unsuspecting Danira. But an excellent choice, I had to admit. *"Manzana carnal."* That was Danira, all right.

"I don't understand this shit," Danira sobbed, snatching the pages from me, "I can't read Spanish."

"I'll translate it for you." I didn't have the heart to tell her what Juan Tomás had done.

"Forget it! I just want to get him out of my system!"

"Listen to me," I said, taking her by the shoulders. "We're going to build a fire on the beach. We'll burn all the poems, and that'll be that. We can exorcize him."

"Jerzy, you're a winner," Danira said, her mood suddenly brightening. She dabbed at her eyes and kissed me and giggled. After another bottle of wine, she showed me a book she said Juan Tomás had given her, a paperback edition of the *Bhagavad Gita*. Scrawled on the flyleaf were the words: "I love you eternally, Juan Tomás."

"I hate him!" she screamed, "I hate him!"

"We'll burn the book, too," I said. "Come on. One way or another, we're going to get this joker out of your system."

Fifteen minutes later, after I'd given Danira a good stiff poking—I felt I owed her that much—we trundled down to the beach lugging three orange crates filled with Juan Tomás's books and poetry. We also brought two more bottles of white zinf. We huddled together, wrapped in a blanket, silently passing our bottle of wine back and forth.

After a few moments, we emptied the orange crates on the sand and broke the crates up into kindling. We crumpled Juan Tomás's bogus poetry pages and started a fire. Then we tossed Juan Tomás's books, one at a time, into the flames: *The Bhagavad Gita, The Rig Veda, The Upanishads,* Bergson's *Creative Evolution, The Life Divine* by Sri Aurobindo, *El Retorno de Los Brujos, The Philosophy of Rabindranath Tagore* by S. Radakrishnan, *The Confessions of Saint Augustine,* in Spanish, *The Sivadvaita of Srikantha, Behind the Cosmic Curtain* by Swami Rudrananda, *The Doctrine of Maya, A Catechism of Hindu Dharma, In Search of the Miraculous* by P. D. Ouspensky, and *All and Everything* by Georges Ivanovitch Gurdjieff.

"Goodbye, Juan Tomás!" Danira shrieked. Her mood had changed abruptly. She was elated now, euphoric even, and her euphoria seemed to be fanning the flames. Book after book she snatched up, ripped apart and tossed into the conflagration, while peals of crazy laughter bubbled from her lips. "It's the end," she howled. "It's the end of everything!"

Into the flames went *The Doctrine of Karma, The Light of Bhagavata, Siddhartha* by Hermann Hesse, *The Nectar of Devotion* by A. C. Bhaktivedanta, *The Breath of God* by Swami Chetanananda, *Samadhi: the Superconsciousness of the Future,* and *The Unobstructed Universe.*

I gazed up at the stars, crawling like lice across the sky,

then out at the sea heaving beyond the twinkling lights of the Santa Monica pier. You could hear the foaming, gentle waves lapping softly at the shore. I kissed Danira again and again. I loved the violence of her doomsday mood, the craziness, the extravagance of it. I handed her the books and she tossed them into the flames—*The Masters and the Path*, *The Tao Teh Ching*, *The Third Eye* by T. Lobsang Rampa, *The Gospel of Sri Ramakrishna*, *The Masks of God*, *Yestermorrow*, *Jacob Boehme: His Life and Teaching*, *Vishnu Purana*, *The Prophet* by Khalil Gibran, *The Tibetan Book of the Dead*, and *The Way of Zen* by Alan Watts.

They made a cheery little fire.

17

I PICKED UP FIFTY BUCKS spinning a sign for Kelly's Copy Shop. It wasn't exactly a cakewalk either, because it was hotter than hell inside that leprechaun costume. First, I stepped into the pants, which were attached to an inflated plastic donut that went around my waist. Then I put on the shoes, big boots with curled up toes, Aladdin shoes, then the shirt and the gloves, and finally the leprechaun's gigantic head, which reached all the way down over my shoulders.

My eyes didn't fit the leprechaun's eyeholes. Instead I had to peer out through a wire grate that was partially hidden by a wispy white beard. I could only see what was right in front of me, and kids would come up behind me and give me a shove, or kick me in the ass. A dog even pissed on my leg.

Next morning, I went to Clifton's for breakfast. I felt I deserved it after cooking for eight hours inside that infernal leprechaun rig. I got the special: Spanish omelet, biscuits, hash browns. $5.98. After breakfast I guzzled a few beers at Jack's Placita. I had money in my pocket and was determined to spend it foolishly. I'd recently learned from Mrs. Egg Roll that Danira had checked herself into the Alcoholism Center for Women on Alvarado, so Danira was out of the question. Besides, I'd already had my big inning with her, and I wasn't looking to extend my hitting streak. I knew perfectly well that if I got hooked up with her again, she'd eventually throw me underneath a bus. At this stage of the game I was like a mosquito that had managed to tank up and flit away without getting squashed. Sometimes it's better to quit while one is ahead.

Suddenly, I got the idea that the Coronet Bar, Beverly and La Cienega, might be just the place to blow off steam, as well as a little cash. It was all the way at the other end of town, but I had time on my hands, and on my side. After another beer, I walked over to Seventh and took the #21 up Wilshire.

At Flower Street, a girl in a red dress with shining ass-length brown hair got on the bus and stood next to my seat. She had a horse-like face and a faint black mustache. Her perfume was intoxicating.

"*Quiere sentarse?*" I ventured, catching her eye.

"*Voy a bajar muy pronto, pero… gracias. Usted es muy amable.*"

The bus lurched, and this Rapunzel, with her magical hair, pressed herself against me. A few strands of her hair flew into my mouth.

Alvarado Street. She gets off the bus and looks back, her eyes meeting mine. The bus lunges forward. Why in God's name didn't I get off? Follow her? Talk to her? *Always a step behind!*

I get off at Park View. Maybe it's not too late. I trot back toward Alvarado, but there's no sign of Rapunzel. Back up Wilshire, past the Park Plaza Hotel. In front of the hotel, catering trucks and lighting crews. They're shooting at the Park Plaza, as always.

I stumble into MacArthur Park and pause in front of the Hungarian Freedom Fighters obelisk. I'm so revved up I have to stop to check my pulse. After a moment, I plop down on a deserted bench. I want to gather myself, and at the same time I'm hoping vaguely now for an encounter with one of the rich girls from the Otis-Parsons Art School next door to the Park Plaza.

On my bench I find a paper bag filled with stale tortillas. I crumble the tortillas up and toss the scraps to the birds. First pigeons, then sparrows cluster at my feet. I watch a sparrow sharpening its beak on the pavement, intent, alert, ready to pounce on any crumb. A perfect little soldier. It's necessary to have a sharp beak, and sharp claws too, if one is to survive in LA.

After a few moments, a street girl approached me. Plaid scarf, tweed cape, army fatigue shirt, at least five sweaters, black leggings, torn denim shorts, mismatched sneakers, windblown blonde hair. Automatically, I dug into my pocket, but she held up a bony hand, shiny with ground-in dirt.

"You shouldn't feed the birds," she said softly.

"Why not?" I mumbled, still searching my pockets for change.

"People are hungry."

When I looked up, she was gone.

18

"AT LEAST I've been having some good nightmares lately."

This was a remark made by a sculptor friend of mine just a few days before he lost his mind. And recently, I can say that the same thing is true of myself. I've been having a recurring dream: Bill Sargent and I are in the prep room, getting ready to embalm a corpse. The man's head is resting on a rubber block. The hydraulic table is slightly tilted so that the blood will flow into the table gutters and wash down the drain. The concrete floor is clean, wet, antiseptic, freshly mopped. The instruments are ready: forceps, scalpel, aneurysm hook, trocar, and injection and drainage valves.

Bill selects a couple of eye caps and inserts them, pulling the lids down over the tiny barbs. He staples the mouth closure wires to the gums and deftly twists them, locking the jaw, then tucks in the ends of the wires. He smears Vaseline over the frozen lips and eyelids.

"He shouldn't give us any trouble."

After studying the corpse for a moment, Bill picks up a scalpel from the tray and quickly makes an incision in the throat, just above the collarbone. He separates the yellow tissue with a forceps, raises the jugular vein, and ties it off.

Then, humming softly to himself, he raises the carotid artery and does the same with it. He makes a longitudinal incision in the jugular and inserts the drainage valve. He inserts the injection valve in the carotid and plugs the valve into a length of surgical tubing that goes to a pump.

The action of the pump will force the embalming fluid from the machine into the carotid artery, and the blood will be forced out the jugular vein. Throughout the process, Bill and I will massage the hands and feet of the corpse to make sure the fluid is working through all the veins and capillaries. A part of my job will be to watch the stream of blood flowing into the gutters, keeping an eye out for 'chicken fat', white clots of cholesterol. If a lot of them show up, we'll have to massage extra hard, or maybe lighten up on the pressure, in order to avoid blowing out a blood vessel.

"Give me half a bottle of the Neo-Pyramid," Bill says. "Fill the rest with water."

I pick up a bottle of embalming fluid and dump half of it into the glass hopper on top of the pump. Bill always starts off with a weak mixture. It takes Bill at least two hours to embalm a body, but he rarely makes a mistake. The other embalmers, Van, Palmer Coldwell and Dick Gregg, mix it 'hot' and finish in twenty minutes. But they have each had corpses go bad on them—skin slip—and Palmer has had several go bad.

I start the pump, keeping my eyes on the flow of blood that's streaming over the man's chest and draining into the gutters. No clots so far. The whir of the motor drones on. Wisps of organ music reach my ears. Van's tuning up in the chapel, "None but the Lonely Heart." He's in a sentimental mood, four sheets to the wind already, most likely. Here's hoping he doesn't get romantic later on.

Bill is wiping his bloody hands on his white apron. "Mix me another batch, will you? A little hotter this time."

I mix it; we shoot it. The corpse is beginning to take on a pink glow, like a mold filling with Jello, as the fluid permeates the tissues.

Suddenly I notice something. The dead man's eyes are open. They're looking at me.

"Holy Jesus," Bill whispers. "This joker's still alive!"

"For God's sake, shut off the pump!" I shout.

Bill looks at me, his face strange, empty, melting away like a lozenge. "It's too late..." His voice echoes through the morgue, and now I hear the organ again. Van, upstairs in the chapel, is leaning on the crescendo pedal, and the rolling thunder of "Valencia" is ringing in my ears.

AT LINDENDAHL'S MORTUARY my main responsibility at night was to answer the phone. I slept in the cosmetics room adjoining the morgue, which was where we dressed and laid out the bodies. I had a bunk, a footlocker and a wall locker, exactly like a soldier. There was also a refrigerator, which I shared with Van in the early days, then with Gray Smallwood, the new night manager, and Palmer Coldwell. It was a pretty good deal if you didn't mind the corpses—the silent ones, perfectly formal and polite, laid out on church trucks with noiseless rubber wheels. Nights when the morgue was full I'd have five or six of them in the cosmetics room with me.

If I got a death call, I'd ring Gray Smallwood, upstairs, and tell him I was going out in the hearse to pick up a body. After getting dressed and chugging a cup of coffee, I'd phone the embalmer on call for that particular night, either Palmer Coldwell, who also lived in the mortuary, or Bill Sargent. Dick Gregg, the Funeral Director, took his turn too. There were four embalmers; they worked rotating shifts. I was the only unlicensed man, except for Raul, who drove the flower truck and did the grounds keeping.

The job was okay, but I missed Van.

Van—Gershon Van Voorhoees—was, at first glance, an undertaker's undertaker, a snazzy dresser with a soft, carefully modulated voice. But there were certain flaws.

His hair was a trifle too long, when you looked close, plus he was swishy and always a little drunk.

Early in life Van had studied for the ministry, but his first love was music. He liked to get sloshed on Crown Royal and play the chapel organ after hours. He'd taught music at a private school in Louisiana and was fired for seducing a boy. He'd also been fired from several funeral parlors for drinking on the job. But there was still a little life left in Van, and that was what I liked about him. He had an air of decadence about him, an air of fatalism that was appealing, as though he'd played the piano for pennies in shoddy New Orleans bars, which was in fact the case.

It was eerie, and also somewhat comical, nights when I was downstairs in the prep room with Palmer Coldwell or Bill Sargent, working over a fresh corpse, to hear the wild peals of "Valencia" rocking the building right off its chocks.

Other nights, when Van was the embalmer on call, it might be two in the morning, and we're just wrapping up a case, when Palmer Coldwell would come strolling into the morgue, stone drunk and eating a carne asada burrito and wanting to talk baseball; and then, after giving Palmer the slip, Van and I would go up to the chapel, and Van would seat himself comfortably in front of the ranks of gleaming pipes and stops and banked keyboards.

With his bottle of Crown Royal at his side, his rimless glasses magnifying his watery blue eyes and a black cigarette holder clamped between his perfect teeth, Van was transformed. He'd roll up his sleeves and go at it like a truck driver, briskly working the pedals with his shoeless feet. To Van, playing the organ was work.

Usually, after warming up with "Faithfully Yours", he'd glide effortlessly into the big hits of the thirties: songs like "Stompin at the Savoy," "Nola," and "Deep Purple." In a sentimental mood, he'd play "Among My Souvenirs," as well as a terrifying rendition of "Boulevard of Broken Dreams." Later, when he got sloppy drunk, he would play

"None But The Lonely Heart."

But Van's tour de force was "Valencia". The building would actually shudder. I walked in on him one night as he sat at the keyboard furiously working the pedals with his black-silk stockinged feet, framed by the heavy velvet curtains that separated the organ pit from the empty chapel. His black coat, carefully folded as always, lay on the carpet. His bottle of Crown Royal was on the bench beside him. This was his finest hour, his moment of crazy drunken triumph, Gershon Van Voorhoees at the keyboard, with his rolled-up sleeves and his fatal smile, clamping his cigarette holder, rocking and sweating like a teamster, stomping on the pedals and double-clutching up eight and a half octaves, stacking the polyphonic choruses higher and higher, chorus upon towering chorus, tier upon tier, up and up and up, as the gigantic, thunderous peals of "Valencia" surged to a victorious, ear-splitting climax.

Palmer Coldwell was the embalmer I worked with most often. Because Palmer lived in the mortuary, he'd frequently take a case for the other fluid-pushers if they were too drunk or too sleepy to take it.

I'm thinking about a particular case Palmer and I did together, a young girl that had come from an autopsy at Good Samaritan. She was ripped open stem to stern, exactly like a steer. Her chest cavity was empty, the skin folded back over her breasts. A section of the ribs had been sawed out. There was an inch or two of blood sloshing around in the empty chest hole.

"Andy Pettite's pitching tonight," Palmer said casually. "He's from Texas, you know. Deer Park. They say he ratted Clemens out, but I don't believe it. I don't see what's wrong with it anyway. Shit, if they can pump cows full of steroids, why not baseball players?"

He glanced at me, then at the plastic bucket that contained the girl's intestines. The top of her head had been sawed off and her brains, a pinkish jelly, were floating around on top of the mess.

"Get a scalpel and chop up them intestines, Hotshot. Then pour some cavity fluid over them. Use a whole bottle. She's ripe!"

Palmer left, and I went about my work. The reason for puncturing the viscera is so that the cavity fluid, formaldehyde primarily, will mix with all the tissues and preserve them. When the mess has been thoroughly 'cooked', we dump it back into the chest hole. Sometimes it happens that the pathologist will keep a lung, or the spleen, or the liver, or a section of the ribs at the hospital for further testing and there isn't enough bulk left to fill out the body properly. In such cases we make up the difference with #10 cotton batting, or old newspapers, or anything that's handy. Usually, we pour the brains in along with it. That makes things more uniform when it comes to fixing up the head.

The heads we stuff with a substance akin to plaster of Paris. We dump the brains back into the skull, but again, the problem frequently is that we don't get enough bulk back from the hospital, which makes the head 'light', and it can sometimes pop up off the pillow while the body is in the coffin, and in the middle of a service, that can be rather embarrassing. The plaster is heavy, and it keeps the head on the pillow.

Palmer came back into the morgue, munching a bean burrito.

"It's over! The Yankees beat their asses. Jesus, I wish I could have seen that shot by A-Rod! Can that boy tee off or what?"

I finish stirring the mess in the stop bucket and stand watching while Palmer expertly packs the thoracic cavity with hardening compound. On his signal, I dump the goulash into the chest hole.

Palmer gave me the job of sewing up. After watching me long enough to satisfy himself that everything was under control, he peeled off his gloves and tossed them into the basket, then he took off his bloodstained apron, stuffed it in the hamper, and left.

Whew! I felt as if a stone had been rolled away from my tomb. Lazarus, come forth! It's a beautiful world without Palmer Coldwell. Humming to myself, I threaded the curved needle and began just below the girl's navel, a simple overhand loop, the baseball stitch, tucking the seams under. Sewing up is pleasant manual work, and best of all it allows your mind to freewheel. It's not so bad, being a body-washer. You're in out of the elements and nobody's standing over you. The undertaking business isn't a bad gig, compared with swinging a pick or unloading trucks or delivering handbills.

A few minutes later Palmer returned, munching a BLT and wearing a ten-gallon hat. He'd discarded his coat and tie, but he'd retained his blood-smeared blue dress shirt and had exchanged his suit pants for a pair of skin-tight jeans. Off duty, Palmer dressed western style: the big white man from Texas with his Tony Lama boots.

With Palmer was Bill Sargent, an old-time embalmer from the gravity-flow days, a Vietnam veteran who had survived a Vietcong POW camp.

"Nice job," Bill commented, leaning on the table.

Palmer's face is contorted with excitement. "Schoenewies is going for the Mets tomorrow at Dodger Stadium," he shouts, stomping his feet like a flamenco dancer. "That's good for LA. His elbow's all fucked up. They'll knock his young Jewboy ass out of the box in the first inning!"

Palmer's face... I forgot to mention about his face. The paralysis... I'd gotten so used to working with him over the months that I hardly noticed it anymore. The facial paralysis was the result of a stroke and affected only his left side. The right side of his face was wonderfully mobile. He mugged it up like a TV star. The eyebrow soared, the eye darted, the nostril dilated, the half-mouth grinned, leered, scowled. But the left side of his face was frozen and stiff, like a face in a wax museum.

It was strange to see half of Palmer's face light up when he got an inspiration, or when something struck him as funny. Animation contrasted with the numbness, I mean. Sometimes, when he got very excited, the dead side would galvanize with a tremendous effort—a spasm, a tic, the smile reflex. When he was tired, the dead side—the Madame Toussaud face—drooped: the left eyelid sagged, the upper lip slumped over his chin, the wax melted: nose, jowl, eyebrow…

A few minutes later, the Old Man appeared with Dick Gregg, the Funeral Director, in tow. A little parley ensued. We learned that we would soon be getting a family of four that had been killed in a restaurant fire, and Dick Gregg and Bill Sargent were coming on duty to take up some of the slack.

The Old Man, Mr. Lindendahl, was a gold-plated success. He was of the old school, like Bill Sargent, harkening back to the days of house calls and gravity-flow embalming. Like every undertaker, Mr. Lindendahl fancied himself as a cosmetician, but his 'faces' were not in a class with Van's, or even Dick Gregg's faces. The man spread color like Matisse. He laid the rouge on thick—a heavy impasto effect. It looked like something that had been done with a trowel. Mr. Lindendahl's faces looked like tropical sunsets.

To watch the Old Man ingratiating himself with a particularly well-heeled family was an illuminating experience. On such occasions, even though I had no business being there, I'd sometimes follow Mr. Lindendahl upstairs to the showroom and loiter around, making a pretense of dusting off the coffins. I liked to watch the Old Man make his pitch. He was an undertaker's undertaker, suave beyond words. His manner was coy and sweet, scarcely concealing a submerged hysteria. It was curious, this sense of panic that lurked just beneath the veneer of his personality. It was almost as if he realized that he was in fact a dead man, and it was that realization that he didn't quite know how to deal with.

The "Deluxe Bronze Sealer Sell" was a well-oiled routine that never varied. Dick Gregg, the Funeral Director, would usher the family in and soften them up a bit while Mr. Lindendahl waited in the darkened alcove just off the softly-lighted showroom, sweetening his breath with a little Sen-Sen.

Dick Gregg, although he performed his duties efficiently, was plainspoken, and far too honest to make a good salesman. He lacked the finesse that Mr. Lindendahl possessed in abundance. But together they made a great one-two punch.

Dick Gregg, after leading the family to the long row of sparkling bronze sealers and performing his spadework, would do a practiced fade, and then the Old Man would close in for the kill. It was a fascinating thing to watch because at full tilt, gliding noiselessly across the thick carpet, his pink face glowing like a wrinkled light bulb, the Old Man looked exactly like one of his own creations.

Bill Sargent was different from the others. He was a dead man, but he wasn't dead in the same way that Mr. Lindendahl was dead, or that Palmer Coldwell was dead. Bill was different. His death had occurred ages ago, and it was final. Presumably, it happened during the war, in the Vietcong POW camp.

Bill Sargent had an air about him that made him seem like the sole survivor of a great catastrophe. He was a man to whom the worst has already happened. I always felt, whenever I worked with Bill, that he could just as well have been flipping hamburgers or throwing pizzas as stuffing corpses, and it would have been the same to him. He showed up for reveille, as it were, but he wasn't attached to his work. Yet he performed his work very well. It was always a pleasure to assist Bill, to watch him apply himself, to see him slugging away elbow-deep in entrails. He went at it like a plumber. For some reason, I've always felt an affinity with those who tinker with the internal hookups and juggle around with the subterranean plumbing of the world, workers such as sandhogs, boiler tenders, safe crackers, coal miners and urologists, and with all those who burrow and tunnel in the matrix—the human pinworms, the sewer rats and the subway workers and the gastro-intestinal specialists. I was born under that star, the dung-beetle star.

But if I'm a dung beetle, Bill Sargent was a worker ant, an inspired termite. He was one of those patient toilers of the earth who tunnel the rivers, clamp the leaks, weld the joints, splice the cables, tap the veins, fuse the thermocouples and scrape and paint the girders, who blow the safes, massage the colons and stack the lethal ant eggs in clean, neat piles. Unlike the others, Bill Sargent never allowed himself to become embroiled in the constant backbiting and petty political intrigues that went on at the funeral parlor. There was something missing from his psyche, it's true; something had been erased, something had been eradicated forever. But whatever the war cut out of Bill Sargent, whatever it was that he left behind him in Vietnam, I couldn't help feeling that he was better off without it.

ONE DAY I'LL NEVER FORGET was the day Van got his walking papers.

In keeping with Van's aura of decadence, with his nostalgia, was the restoration work he specialized in. Van's cosmetic work was good. Van was an artist through and through. He had a light touch, and he exercised a good deal of restraint. Paradoxically, it was a faulty wax job that led to his getting canned. The incident took place just two months after his arrival. Half of the man's face had been blown away by a self-inflicted shotgun blast. Van did his usual skillful job of modeling the nose, the lips and one ear out of wax, but somehow he failed to attach the thing securely enough to what was left of the dead man's face. During the Rosary, the widow leaned over the coffin and kissed her husband's cheek, and the wax job came away and stuck to her lips. She collapsed on the floor. I quickly gathered her up and cracked an ammonia crystal under her nose.

Instantly, she came to, babbling cheerfully: "Mommy, I'm home from school! Happy birthday, Mommy! Happy birthday!"

Her mind was gone. I had to call an ambulance. The upshot of it was that Van got the axe.

Months later, a few days before I left the job at Lindendahl's myself, we got ourselves a homecoming queen, killed in a car wreck on high school graduation night, a beautiful girl, hardly a mark on her. The impact snapped her neck, clean as a whistle. After Palmer and I got her embalmed and dressed and all, it was time for the application of the cosmetics. This stage was Palmer's favorite; it was his vocation, his métier. Palmer considered himself a master cosmetician, a regular Bottecelli when it came to the restoration work.

It followed quite naturally then, when it came to the cosmetics, that we had to adjourn for coffee, to "talk things over." During this intensive briefing, which was conducted at Denny's, Palmer went into his subject with brisk thoroughness and astonishing bravura.

"The eyebrows are very important," he informs me confidentially, "You can change the whole...character...of a face by just arching the eyebrows a little bit. Notice I said, 'a little!' Just a smidge! That's the whole secret of it...knowing when to stop. The cheekbones are important too. Don't forget that!"

Here comes the waitress, bouncing her tits, pretty cute, she takes our order. As she's walking away, Palmer stares appraisingly at her ass. This provokes some interesting little twitches in the dead left side of his face.

"Not bad," he says parenthetically. "How'd you like to git you some of that, Hotshot?"

He leans across the table, drumming urgently with his

fingers. "Now you take her cheekbones... They're way too flat. See what I mean? You'd want to build 'em up a little bit. You never want to be afraid to shoot you a little tissue-filler under the surface. Gives you a firmer texture... That's important! And you always want to use the powder, too, after you finish up. It helps to tone down the high spots. Now you take Dick Gregg," he says. "Dick don't always remember to use the powder, and it shows. You know what I mean?"

He lowers his voice and leans over the table, almost falling in my lap. "El Dico had an eye pop open on him a couple weeks ago, you know. Lucky that Bill Sargent was on duty that night. Lucky for Dick, I mean. He's a good man, Bill. Always checks out the slumber rooms before a Rosary. He's right on the job, you know? Damn lucky thing, too. He really saved old Dick's ass..."

Then, parenthetically, breathing through his fist, larding his words with sarcasm and malice, "Say, what's wrong with that boy, anyhow? He walks around with his head up his ass half the time. Acts like he's got something bothering him, you know what I mean? He was crocked to the gills the other morning at graveside, too, out at Evergreen. Lucky for him the Old Man wasn't along on that one!"

Suddenly, in an enterprising tone, Palmer blurts: "You know, Hotshot, if you toe the line, watch your p's and q's, the Old Man might just put you through embalming school down there at Cypress, like he did Dick Gregg. That's how Dick got his start, you know. He walked in one day, off the street, just like you, and the Old Man took a liking to him."

Sitting there, half listening to Palmer, I'm smiling to myself as I think of the stylized doll-like beauty of the women's faces that Palmer has made up. In fact, it never mattered to Palmer what they looked like to begin with, how old they were or how shot through with wrinkles, pitted, scowling like Neanderthal women, always he made them over into The Face. It was the face of a plastic doll, beautiful, soulless, like the molded plastic death mask of Queen Nefertiti. The lips were unnaturally bright, the cheeks rosy as apples, and the eyebrows glittered like twin Golden Gate Bridges. It was eerie, and I'm putting it mildly, to see them all turn out the same way.

She, The Face, was a genuine mythical being made visible by Palmer's artistry. She was the Birth of Venus, Goddess of Beauty, served up on the half shell with plenty of catsup and horseradish. She was the absolute monarchess of the beauty that's stamped out in job lots, of the eternal and imperishable Egyptian loveliness that is animated by cold music and warm death.

Here we are back at the funeral home, Palmer and I. Two days have passed, and the girl's family, predictably, has complained about Palmer's cosmetic work. Palmer is in a snit. In fact, he is positively livid.

"Jesus H. Christ! Goddamn it! What's the matter with these people, anyway? Just who do they think they are? Where do they get off telling me what to do?"

And on and on, like that. He'd made her beautiful, hadn't he? What more did they want? To prove his point, he whips out the photograph the family had brought in earlier to serve as a guide for the cosmetic work.

"Well, what do you think?" he demands. He shows me the photo, close up, then steps quickly to the coffin and executes a Dali-esque flourish with his stubby arm.

"Now look at...this! Now there's...beauty! Look at the cheeks. See the pink skin tones? Look at them lips. Real lifelike! Am I the Man or what? Look at the eyelids. Take a look at the position of the hands. That's not something you learn in five minutes! And they want to tell me! That's what burns my ass! What the hell do they know? Look... Take a good look at this...in the coffin... Now there's beauty for you! Well? Well? What about it? How'd you like to git you some of that, Hotshot?"

19

I CAME INTO SOME CASH. My maiden aunt in Vermont heard I was trying to be a writer and sent me three hundred dollars. I decided that a little vacation was in order. I now had an opportunity to get away from Ysela and to stop thinking about her, if I could. I'd realized by this time that she wasn't about to pick up and go to Zihuatanejo with me, so I would go to Zihuatanejo alone. Zihuatanejo! The Real Mexico...

I knew it was foolish, this business about "the Real Mexico." What I wanted was to get away from Ysela and away from the border for a while. I wanted to hear Spanish spoken exclusively. I wanted to sit at the foot of a mountain on the terrace of a café where the waiter brings your tequila sunrise an hour or two after you've forgotten you ordered it. I wanted to listen to the soft melodious tinkle of Spanish in my ears, Spanish and only Spanish. I wanted to immerse myself—in Spanish, in forgetfulness, in anonymity. In Mexico you don't have to *be* anybody, you don't have to *do* anything to prove that you're worthy to draw breath. You simply *are*. And people congratulate you for it. It's enough, it suffices, it satisfies. To be, to exist. In Mexico it's a triumph, a victory. It's something to be glad about.

The day I got the check from Aunt Mizpah I went to the Tango Club to think things over. I rarely went to the Tango Club, and only then because of the music. They had Edith Piaf on the jukebox. The girls wore phantom leather jackets, black lipstick, high boots and short skirts. They were loud, coarse, stunning. Most of the clientele were *Alemánes*, German NATO exchange officers stationed at Fort Bliss, arrogant shits who dressed like European hoodlums. The rest were American doggies. I was the only one who didn't fit, as usual. The Tango Club was a rotten hole in the wall, and I hated it—except for the music.

At the Tango Club I had a few Carta Blancas and played Piaf, *"Toujours Aimer."* I tried to get the attention of one of the fluff-girls, a sullen little number with a black leather vest and an Iron Cross nestled between her tits, but she gave me a contemptuous glance and spat on the floor. Meaning that she preferred to wait for one of the storm troopers, a Kraut with a big bankroll and a big schwantz.

I ordered another Carta and glanced again at Aunt Mizpah's letter:

"Dear Jerzy, the ice is melting on Lake Bomoseen..."

I finished my beer and left the Tango. I bought a bottle of Cuervo Gold and checked into a hotel on Avenida Juárez. I could afford it, certainly, and I wanted some peace and quiet in which to mull things over—about the trip, I mean—my prospective journey to the Real Mexico.

In my room I poured myself a drink. After one drink I decided to take a bath. In the bathtub I reread a passage I'd underlined in a book I'd been carrying around with me, *The Maze and the Minotaur* by John Calvin Ryder:

"The unraveling of the thread that leads to the heart of the labyrinth is a journey of rediscovery. The clues that we vaguely recognize, the handwriting on the walls, the tentative fingers that point and crumble to dust, are emblems of a circuitous voyage. Our destination is secret, but not unknown. The course is uncharted, yet certain and fixed. The answer that we seek is not distant, but near.

The equation is simple rather than complex. The Minotaur—and the maze itself—are nothing more than an elaborate subterfuge that we have invented in order to disguise the obvious. It is as if we must circumnavigate the globe in order to arrive at our own doorstep."

Interesting, very interesting. Somehow my mood for going to Zihuatanejo had fled. For one thing, I was dead tired. I'd hardly slept the previous night, fretting about Ysela and trading punches in my mind with "El Indio" Mendoza. Maybe after a night's sleep, I told myself, turning a page. But I knew the danger of that. If I waited a day I'd hook up again with Ysela, we'd go on a spree, the three hundred dollars would be gone, and goodbye Zihuatanejo. So I got out of the tub, dried off and got dressed. *Zihuatanejo, here I come!*

On the way to the bus station I stopped at a *farmacia* to buy a new toothbrush, my only luggage besides my bottle of Jose Cuervo and *The Maze and the Minotaur*. Clothes? I'd buy a change of clothes when I got there, I told myself, something sporty, something tropical. But when I arrived at the station I discovered that it was still five hours until the next bus for Zihuatanejo, so I stepped into the street. *Five hours to kill.*

I considered going back to the hotel, but then I remembered that I'd already checked out. I knew one thing. I had a wad of bills that was burning a hole in my pocket. Suddenly, I realized I was lost. I'd been wandering aimlessly, *thinking*. The crooked streets, the leering huts, the serape-bundled figures, the smoking fires—all had been daubed by a madman with a few quick brush strokes on a muddy canvas. The cadmium yellow moonlight flowed like rich gravy over the roofs of the houses. In the rutted streets it glowed with the texture of burlap.

Gradually, I realized that I was headed south on the road toward Colonia San Felipe del Real, eventually to intersect Sixteenth of September Street. Off to my left was the sprawl of Ciudad Juárez; behind me lay the glittering bowl of El Paso surmounted by the gigantic stone Christ,

El Cristo Rey, his outstretched arms piercing the tall plumes of black smoke rising from Smeltertown.

I paused and reread the passage from Ryder, as if I were consulting a map.

"The clues that we vaguely recognize, the handwriting on the walls, the tentative fingers that point and crumble to dust, are emblems of a circuitous voyage..."

Emblems of a circuitous voyage... Great title! I jotted it down, on the back of Aunt Mizpah's letter.

Then I remembered. This was the route I followed from Colonia Alta Vista to Mariscal Street, in the early days, when I was living at Monalisa's with Roscoe and the in-laws. It wasn't a direct route, by any means, but it was a definite one. I went the same way every time. There were certain landmarks, certain huts that differed, however slightly, from the others, certain junctions where I turned, doglegged, zigzagged. And there were faces, young girls, very shy, who lived with their families, but staring, whenever I walked past, always in certain windows, saying everything with their eyes. In Mexico, it's the eyes that predominate. In Mexico, everyone is *watching.*

"The course is uncharted, yet certain and fixed."

I plunged headlong into the maze of mud huts, striking out at first in the general direction of Mariscal Street, but then, on impulse, I began purposely making wrong turns, going down streets I'd never walked before, places I'd never been. In my mind was the image of the labyrinth; in the center, the Minotaur's lair. Never had Juárez seemed so mysterious, so hallowed, as if each adobe hut were a transparent skull lit up by a single feverish candle. Ciudad Juárez was the holy city, a citadel, more magical and shimmering than New Jerusalem. I was beginning to hallucinate from lack of sleep, and I was enjoying every minute of it.

A few hours later I was standing at the bar of a cantina on the edge of the red-light district with a tequila in my paw and my wad of bills bursting like a nugget of radium in my pocket. In my mind, I was walking the cobblestones of Zihuatanejo. I was in Ixtapa, sitting with Aunt Mizpah by the pool at the Hotel El Presidente, and the sun was shining. The tray of iced drinks arrived, and the nachos and *jalapeños* and the chilled slices of papaya bathed in lime juice. I saw the stone arches of Cabo San Lucas rising up out of the ocean like gates to the Sea of Cortez. I was eating lobster under a thatched-roof palapa while a marimba band played on the shore. I saw the lean-tos of the shark hunters at Magdalena Bay, and the great green sea turtles. And in Mulegé, the bare-breasted women were washing their long silky hair in the jungle river that flows into Bahia de la Concepción. Mexico, the Real Mexico. It's beautiful. *And I've still got five hours until I catch the bus...*

Moments later, walking again, I paused at La Calle Noche Triste, the Street of the Sad Night, such an inviting spot that one almost feels an obligation to loiter. Leaning against a pockmarked wall under a torn bullfight poster, facing the cathedral, I watched an American crossing the street. I recognized that walk. And he was carrying a folded newspaper. It was Roscoe. I was certain of it. Instinctively, I ducked into a doorway. Seconds later, peering around a *"Dentista"* sign, I watched the man, who looked nothing at all like Roscoe, disappear into a bar.

Hallucinations...

A few steps further and I found myself in front of the Restaurant Palenque, where hundreds of naked chickens were roasting on spits over troughs brimming with yellow grease. The menu was painted in red letters on the window. An exhaust fan whirled above the door, pumping heavenly aromas into the street. Inside, women in papery white dresses were rolling balls of dough on wooden boards and patting them into tortillas. Behind the women enormous ovens breathed like ravenous beasts. Sumptuous roasts and stupendous joints of fragrant roasted meat dangled on hooks among black iron pots and copper pans while doll-like *meseras* hurried with gigantic platters of chicken, roasted pork and *cabrito*. Mexico is a workers' epic, a renaissance of the senses, a folk-opera dedicated to the belly.

I buy a taco from a pushcart vendor. Leaning against a wall, I reread Aunt Mizpah's letter. Suddenly, I'm in Vermont, sitting at Aunt Mizpah's kitchen table. It's late summer—no, it's autumn, the leaves are turning to crimson and orange and the perch are biting like crazy at Lake Bomoseen. The Franklin stove is glowing cherry red and I've just finished cleaning the fish. We're drinking hard cider and Aunt Mizpah is writing me one of her long literary letters which she doesn't have to send because I'm there with her, with Aunt Mizpah, in Green Vermont.

"The Minotaur—and the maze itself—are nothing more than an elaborate subterfuge that we have invented in order to disguise the obvious. It is as if we must circumnavigate the globe in order to arrive at our own doorstep."

Walking again, along *Calle Ugarte*. Here the bricks, softly eroded like weathered bread, are slimed over with a thin plaster-wash of bile-green paint. Pushcarts squat on automobile tires in the rutted mud, and beggar children huddle in front of tiny *loncherías* whose menus are chalked on slates propped outside the door.

Calle Ugarte—I feel it through the middle, in the solar plexus—a tunnel that pierces my navel. *Calle Ugarte* is an umbilical street that connects me in an alimentary way, in a flesh-and-blood way, with Mexico. On *Calle Ugarte*, Mexico is alive. Mexico the garbage scow, Mexico the fountain of inhuman longings, Mexico, a sow with a billion tits. Mexico, Mother of the World. Mexico! *Mexico siempre!*

Of course I missed the bus. At some moment during the night I remembered. I made it to the station, but the bus had already pulled out.

"How long until the next bus?" I inquired at the window.

"Five hours, señor."

Of course! Five hours, señor!

175

Needless to say, I went back to Mariscal Street. More Carta Blancas, more frenzied wandering through the passageways of the labyrinth. At some ungodly hour of the morning, as though I'd been drawn there by unconscious design, blindly unraveling some finespun thread, I found myself once again in front of the Tango Club. Was this the heart of the maze? The Minotaur's lair? I sauntered inside. The place was dead, except for a single German officer seated at the bar and a humpbacked flower vendor sleeping in a booth near the toilet. The whores were waiting in a row, slumped against the wall, sullenly asleep. As I approached the bar, the German swiveled on his stool. He had a shaved head and a bull neck.

"*Wie geht's?*" he muttered, his eyes ice-blue slots in a mask. As he slid off his stool I noticed that he was a little shorter than I am, but terrifically compact and muscular. I had the distinct impression that he was inhumanly powerful—and utterly merciless.

"*Wie geht's?*" I responded, automatically shaking his proffered hand. I'm was on my toes, ready for action, but the German, after surveying me for a moment with those edelweiss eyes, smiled enigmatically and returned to his stool.

"A drink for my *Amerikaner* friend," he said to the bartender. "*Was mochten Sie trinken?*"

"*Eine tequila mitt limón, bitte,*" I managed.

I realized now why I'd returned to the Tango Club. Standing with one foot resting on the brass rail, I surveyed the lineup of girls. After deliberating for a moment, I chose one in a short black skirt with pleats, high shiny boots, and an unzipped black phantom leather jacket spangled with *Luftwaffe* emblems and the inevitable Iron Cross dangling between her breasts.

Scrumptious!

I walked over and gave her a nudge, silently holding out a crisp ten-spot.

"*Wie geht's?*"

"Kiss my ass, *guero*."

"I intend to, *meine schatz*," I answered calmly.

My excitement mounted as she coldly took the bill and went to the bar where the bartender was snoozing, rag in hand, behind the cash register. As he sleepily rang up the sale and handed her a roll of toilet paper and a token to put on her key ring, she yawned and stretched, arching her back; she glared at me over her shoulder, then spat on the floor. She was obviously pissed off at being disturbed, not at all in the mood, which excited me even more.

It was gorgeous. I made her leave everything on, the boots, the pleated skirt, the black leather jacket half-unzipped with the Iron Cross nestled between her breasts. While I strained and sweated, she coldly snapped her bubblegum and cursed me bitterly in Spanish, English and German. At the last possible instant I pulled out and came all over her tits, on her face, on her glossy black lipstick, and on the phantom leather jacket spangled with *Wehrmacht* insignia, dangling Hitler *Jungund* medals and silver swastikas. A dirty trick, but I was looking for my ten bucks worth, and I got it.

"*Pinche guey!* Motherfucker! *Cochino marrano!*"

After this treat I sat at a table and ordered a tequila sunrise, as well as a drink for the Kraut at the bar. I fed the jukebox, Piaf, the Sparrow of the Streets, warbling "*Toujours Aimer*." It's beautiful, I thought. *Nothing like this in Vermont!*

Street photographers and beggars strolled past the door, and the Menudo Man, with his steaming kettle and his wooden yoke. I kept depositing my dimes and nickels in the machine, and Piaf's magic voice came soaring out, showering despair and absolution on the early morning pavement.

A hunchback approached me, the flower vendor I'd seen earlier snoozing in the booth near the toilet. I gave the man a ten-dollar bill and told him to go to a nearby restaurant. "Bring three breakfasts," I told him in Spanish.

The hunchback had his son with him, a stunted, dreamy-eyed boy. The man's eyes, when I whipped out that ten-spot, were like saucers. I didn't know whether he'd come back or not, and I didn't care.

An hour later, after I'd forgotten all about the incident, the hunchback brought the plates, *machaca*, heaps of fried potatoes, salad, *refritos*, tortillas and a big bowl of salsa fresca. We all pitched in, the man, the boy and I, dipping our tortillas in the same bowl of salsa. The hunchback eyed me gratefully, as if I were don Benito Juárez himself, while the boy grinned foolishly and ate with his fingers.

Before I'd finished eating I told the bartender to bring me a telephone. I dialed the bus station.

"*A qué hora sale el camión para Zihuatanejo?*" I barked into the receiver. "When is the next bus for Zihuatanejo?" I felt like a *Gran Señor* with all that money in my pocket. It was exhilarating. *Money talks and bullshit walks!*

The answer came back, the answer I'd been expecting, the answer I knew I would receive:

"*Five hours, señor.*"

I bought the bartender a tequila and spread my bills out on the table. I knew I was being scrutinized by the German Minotaur at the bar, but I didn't give a rat's balls.

There it was—everything I had left, one hundred and ninety-five dollars, my vacation in Zihuatanejo. But I knew I wasn't going. I didn't have to leave because I'd already arrived. I was there...in Mexico, the Real Mexico, where the sky is always blue and the tablecloths are white and the silverware always tinkles musically in the background. And the mountain is there, waiting impassively in the distance, and the *mesero* with his tray of iced drinks is perpetually poised just offstage. The Real Mexico...where the drink or the meal arrives hours after you've forgotten you ordered it, and the bus is always five hours late, or else there is no bus, but it doesn't matter. *No le hace.* It doesn't matter.

No le hace. That's the lesson you learn in Mexico. *No le hace.* It doesn't matter. Mexico, the Real Mexico, is a state of mind. You don't go to it. It comes to you. It's a matter of windage and elevation. It's a matter of adjusting your set. The Real Mexico is a state of mind in which you always have five hours until you catch the bus...

20

I'M NOW LIVING in Lafayette Park with Polly Pink Shoes. At night we roost in the cold trees. By day we peck at crumbs in the gutter.

It's funny. One day I was riding the bus to work. When my stop came, I didn't pull the cord. I just sat there, frozen. That's how quickly it happened. There was no conscious decision on my part. As we rolled past Lindendahl's Mortuary, I realized that that period of my life was over. It was eerie, I mean, the non-volitional aspect of it. But I was also floating on air. I was through stuffing corpses for eight bucks an hour. I didn't go back to get my things, or even my paycheck. French leave, as they say. And that black suit! I left it hanging in my locker in the cosmetics room. Fuck it! Better to take one's chances out in the open.

Now I'm living the life of an urban hunter-gatherer—again. Polly Pink Shoes is a real handful. She's 'clinically depressed'. All day long she pours it out; her pain, her suffering, her regret. She loves to enumerate her failures, like a leper who keeps track of how many fingers he's lost. And she's constantly talking suicide. I found her pink shoes on a bus bench one day. I thought surely she'd offed herself. But no, she'd just gone to the toilet. Why did she take off her shoes to go to the toilet? You tell me... She's mad as a hatter, of course. Carries a canary around in a cage. Robert. It's Robert who tests the air each day as she goes down into her personal coal mine.

My stint at Lindendahl's, looking back, was a vegetative period, a long slumber, a dream, *einen nachttraum*. The job itself was tedious, but at least my mind was active, if only in a subterranean way. As if I were putting myself in cold storage for a while.

The mortuary was a labyrinth that I entered as a dung beetle, and from which I emerged, some months later, as Osiris, God of the Dead. Strange as it may sound, the long hours, the crazy crew, the lugubrious surroundings and my macabre duties, far from plunging me into depression, had a beneficial effect on me. The fact is that I thoroughly enjoyed my entombment. Like the dung beetle, I had my comfortable burrow and my ball of sustenance, and like the dung beetle I was happy. Eventually, of course, my Sun God personality began to assert itself. But that was later. For the time being I was more than content to accept my incarceration and to gnaw blissfully away in the darkness like a patient termite. It was as though I were inoculating myself against a virus, the death virus, by swallowing a generous helping of that virus. With each day that passed, and with each funeral I attended, and with each corpse I labored over, I felt myself becoming more indifferent, more immune to despair, and far more certain of my own good fortune, regardless of what uses the world might make of me.

And today the Dung Beetle is alive and well. It's as if my life on Earth is now merely a hobby that I pursue at leisure. Here I am, strolling up and down Broadway without a care in the world. In this detached condition the chipped cornices of a structure like the Fine Arts Building—that Rococo wedding cake—are as fascinating to me as the bouncing breasts of a gorgeous street-stepper prancing along Sunset Boulevard; or if I happen to be ambling along Fifth, in the vicinity of San Pedro or San Julian as twilight cloaks the city canyons, the spectacle of a cursing derelict settling into his filthy cocoon of blackened rags.

I've been trying to teach Polly Pink Shoes how to write a good suicide note. You've got to grab the reader with that first line. Something catchy, like: FUCK YOU AND THE HORSE YOU RODE IN ON! People simply don't have time to read these days, and if you don't have a great hook, then your suicide note will end up in the shredder. Another suggestion: keep it to a single page. Follow your hook up with a brief but informative paragraph: your pain, your disappointment, your despair. Final hint: always leave 'em laughing. End your suicide note with a lighthearted quip, a bawdy joke or a careless jest.

Yesterday was a bad day. Poor little Robert was swaying on his perch. I thought he was going to keel over. Down and down and down we went, into bituminous blackness, pursuing a particularly tedious vein of ore. You couldn't see your hand in front of your face. Plus it was starting to sprinkle and I was getting hungry. I even began thinking about a pepperoni pizza I'd left in the fridge back at the funeral home. And I was thinking too that I'd better get out of this situation with Polly Pink Shoes before I get black lung disease. That's when I got the bright idea of going back to Boyle Heights. Sure, Boyle Heights. Any port in a storm.

Polly Pink Shoes is a pain in the ass, but I can't say anything bad about Robert. At least he's not clinically depressed! Far from it, he's an extraordinarily cheerful little chap. Robert had the good fortune of being born a nitwit. *Twitter, twitter, twitter*, all day long. Robert's a great earner, too. The tourists love him. He sings for them. We park ourselves on a bus bench in front of Bullocks Wilshire and Polly tells them, "I just want to get some birdseed for my canary." And they shell out, believe me. It's beautiful.

Just the same, I pulled stakes and went over to Boyle Heights. I didn't know what I'd find there, but I was not prepared for the catacombs that Jack had created under the building. Ah! Jack has been a busy boy! You talk about a dung beetle... Jack has built an elaborate system of underground rooms bolstered with timbers and boards, a subterranean city, and he carried out every bit of the dirt in his mandibles.

We have an African girl with us now, Naameka. Insane, no English, or Spanish, sleeps all the time, her face distorted and twitching, as if she's reliving the memory of a voyage on a slave ship. She lives in one of the underground rooms.

Other occupants include some chatty Cambodians, a bewildered family from Honduras, humble as field mice, and a geezer with a blind stick who may or may not actually be blind.

Topside, I met Reno Blackey, an old railroad tramp wearing a Third Army overcoat over a black shirt and pants. We shared a bottle of Night Train. *Here comes the train; there goes the pain!* Reno's poison of choice is tokay. "Ever go over the Hump in a tokay blanket?" he asked me. Tokay and Pink Lady. "There's a trick to making Pink Lady, you know," he explained. "You gotta strain your Sterno through a loaf of French bread. Or you can use a flannel rag. You can even use your socks if you have to. But you gotta strain it. A lot of them don't know that, and a lot of them's dead."

Reno Blackey has a grimy negligee that he sleeps with, hugging it to his chest. "Melanie," he calls it. He even kisses it goodnight before he conks off with a blissful expression on his mug. "*Good night, Melanie.*" He insists on sleeping out, under the stars, right next to the campfire. Doesn't talk much except about getting back on Old Dirtyface, riding over to the next division and jungling up. That and: "Me and towns don't mix."

Lon Tidwell was a real person, or at least he had been. I

mean he wasn't into the swill or anything like that. Unlike the rest of us, Lon Tidwell wasn't a dysfunctional person, a drunk or a drug addict, insane, a criminal, a refugee or a revolutionary. Yet, here he was in the Catacombs with his toothbrush in his shirt pocket.

Lon Tidwell was a structural engineer; he had a wife and child. The family's descent to the streets had been rapid, as if they'd fallen down a coal chute. First he lost his job, and then they lost the house, the cars and the credit cards. I felt sorry for these people because they'd never had to rough it before. They were ordinary citizens who'd tried to do the right thing. They voted, held jobs, paid their bills. Now the lot of them—Lon, the wife and the little girl—were living in a hole in the ground with brown recluse spiders and Norwegian rats. There was a new Depression going on out there. Not that it meant anything to guys like Jack and me, but a whole host of ordinary people like the Tidwells were having their asses handed to them.

Now I don't mean to call Jack's creation 'a hole in the ground'. The multi-level, hollowed-out chambers, shored up with timbers, were joined by wooden stairways and plank walkways, and in some places he'd poured concrete, making friendly little grottoes, and he'd laid odd sections of sewer pipe, creating a sophisticated drainage system. It was amazing, a regular Maginot Line. A sparkling achievement, and Jack was the architect of it all. He was the Crown Prince of Third World America: Jack, the slumlord of slumlords.

It was quiet at night except for the midnight train, Old Dirtyface, clattering through the industrial jungle along the Los Angeles River, splitting the night wide open with its demented hooting, carrying everything away, farther and farther, silent then hooting again, and farther, silent and hooting and distant and gone.

Some nights as we'd stand in our dugout peering through the chicken wire at the moon, I'd get an eerie feeling of déjà vu, as if Jack and I had served together in the trenches of World War I, at the Somme or Château-Thierry. I'd hear bullets snapping in the air around our heads, searching for us, and from time to time when twinkling flares lit everything up bright as day you'd see corpses stacked like cordwood, denuded black trees, dead mules and sometimes a gutted horse writhing on the ground. Enemy shells turned somersalts in the air above our heads, and chugging mortars rained dirt and debris down on us; meanwhile the German machine guns on the other side of no man's land were steadily spitting bullets at us, bullets that somehow knew exactly where you were, and where you would be in the next moment.

And now we're fixing bayonets and in a moment we'll be going over the top and the fear is so thick you can cut it with a knife…

My visions were brief, and they came in flashes. I never said anything to Jack about them.

Lon Tidwell and I went out scavenging. I wanted to show him a thing or two. He learned quickly. You do when you're hungry. We'd barge into a restaurant, go up to deserted tables and snag the food off the plates before the busboys could get to it. Lon's clothes were still pretty spiffy, so we had that going for us. We'd stuff the food in our mouths, and we carried plastic bags too. After a while we caught a bus across town and hit a string of eateries on Hollywood Boulevard, blitzkrieg-style. Before anyone knew what was going on, we were sailing out the door.

As we headed back to Boyle Heights, Lon was in an upbeat mood. His stomach was full and so was his plastic bag. He was elated to realize that he could still provide for his family. He grabbed my hand and shook it.

"Thanks, brother," he said.

"You'd do the same for me," I said.

"Damn straight!"

Lon Tidwell was a brave and resourceful guy, and I could tell that he was going to be okay.

ABOUT THE AUTHOR

Donald O'Donovan was born in Cooperstown, New York. A teenage runaway, he rode freights and hitchhiked across America, served in the US Army with the 82nd Airborne Division, lived in Mexico, and worked at more than 200 occupations including telephone psychic, undertaker and roller skate repairman. A former long distance truck driver, he wrote *Confessions of a Bedbug Hauler* while running 48 states and Canada for Schneider National. As a volunteer at the Braille Institute in Los Angeles he recorded several western novels, and subsequently studied voice acting with James Alburger and Penny Abshire. O'Donovan lived for two years at the historic Wilshire Royale Hotel while writing *Tarantula Woman* (Open Books, 2011), and wrote the first draft of *Night Train* (Open Books, 2010) on 23 yellow legal pads while homeless in the streets of LA. An optioned screenwriter and voice actor with film and audio book credits, Donald O'Donovan lives mostly in Los Angeles.